Edj of the Empire

Episode 1: Herrig's World

Timothy Burns

chandra

Books by Timothy Burns

Edj of the Empire: Herrig's World
Edj of the Empire: Revenant's Omen

CHAPTER 1

Coming to consciousness in a trash-strewn alley behind a dive bar on a rough-and-tumble mining world was quite a rude awakening, let me tell you. I suppose it beat the alternative, though - not waking up at all. Not that Sam would've let that happen.

I could tell there would be a knot on the back of my head even before I managed to convince my hand to undertake the monumental task of venturing up there to check it out, and I was right. I didn't expect that hand to come away bloody, but that it did so didn't really surprise me, either.

It had been one of those nights.

I suppose I'd better back up a little bit since I don't know who might end up reading this account. First off, I am Prince Edj Dumarc LaRand Bronacious Tarkle, son of Emperor Risherd Fontanue LaRand Bronacious Tarkle, Crown Prince and Heir to the Crystal Throne of the Empire of the Ninety-Nine Stars.

Yep, that Prince Edj. You might have heard of me, but if not, that's okay. You'd be surprised how many Imperial subjects don't even know they are Imperial subjects, much less who their next monarch will be. And you know what? That doesn't bother me one bit.

See, I know something that all those pompous, overdressed, kowtowing arrogant fools back at my Father's court can't even begin to comprehend: the average person couldn't care less what goes on in the Glittering Palace. What concerns them are their day-to-day affairs, not what's happening light-years away to people they've never met and who think themselves so much better than the commoners that, if they ever did meet them, would treat them like dirt anyway. Less than dirt, really. Dirt has value, while commoners are simply numbers in a database.

I guess that explains what I was doing out there on the very rim of the Empire. I don't have any more to do with those self-important, ego-inflated aristocrats than I absolutely have to. Don't get me wrong, now - I love my father. It's all the fools he's surrounded by I can't stand. And since in an Empire the size of the Ninety-Nine Stars there are always a ton of minor situations that need attention before they become major problems, I can always find reasons to be anywhere other than Alphum.

Like, for instance, on Herrig's World.

I doubt there are more than a dozen people on the whole of the capitol planet who've ever heard of Herrig's World, much less know that the place's only major export is minzite ore. Yet nearly everyone makes use of the antigravity and artificial-gravity generators the refined form of this extremely rare mineral makes possible.

There are any number of products like this, of course, available from only one or a very few sources but highly desired everywhere, in this great Empire of ours. Few, however, are as universally used as minz coils. So, when the production of something as valuable as this experiences a sharp decline for no apparent reason, it attracts attention.

Now, this could have been addressed in several different manners. The navy could have been sent in to investigate, but they never do anything small. A flotilla of a dozen or more starships would have arrived, and chances are production would've suddenly undergone a miraculous recovery. At least until they left, anyway. Or an official auditor could have been dispatched, but he would have found several perfectly good reasons for the decline and filed a report saying, oh well, that's just the way it is. He would be much wealthier by the time he did so, but, well, that's just the way it is.

Or I could go there and make a few quiet, discrete inquiries and find out precisely who was profiting when several different mining corporations all suddenly started reporting record-low production rates.

It sounded so simple when I told my father I'd look into things there. But is anything ever simple?

During the two-week hyperspace flight from the agricultural world Demetria, where I'd just investigated and solved a nasty case of well poisoning, I read up on all I could find about Herrig's World, which wasn't a whole lot. It's a relatively young planet, mostly jungle on its one huge continent, and its native life is at that stage in its evolution where every species is trying out all kinds of creative ways to kill and eat every other species. Think Earth's dinosaur epoch on mega-steroids, because life there found a way to make natural ceramics early on. Everything is armored in super-tough shells, and every creature has its own uniquely lethal means of getting at the delicious creamy filling of these hard shells.

Minzite mining is the sole reason for a human presence there, and temporary mining towns are practically the only settlements on the whole planet. People have been plundering it for something like 400 years now, and they still have to import virtually everything they use there. It seems that a world full of hungry beasts with armor-piercing appendages just doesn't attract many farmers or vacationers. Go figure.

The culture there is just what you'd expect in mining towns surrounded by lethal predators on all sides. Lives are cheap, passions run high, and everyone is armed to the teeth.

Oh, and did I mention the fact that the mines pay so well that, despite all this, people are willing to kill to get hired on?

It's not a place for the weak or timid.

Now you might think that I, being Crown Prince and all of that, would be so un-used to a place like this that I'd faint at the mere mention of such savagery.

Perish the notion.

I thrive on danger. I go out of my way to find situations where I can test my mettle against the worst this universe can throw at me, be it man, beast, or nature itself. I've wrestled a B'norr hyper-gorilla to the ground and bested an entire city full of professional Spak players at their own game. I am anything but weak or timid. I know the galaxy is a dangerous place, and Daddy didn't raise no fool, as the saying goes.

More than a few people have speculated that I have a subconscious death wish. Ha. As if.

What they don't know - what very few outside the Imperial household know - is that I am not allowed to die.

Note to the Imperial historians: since it is on your request that I am committing this record of my travels to permanent storage and you asked that I make it as complete and honest an account as possible, I leave it up to you to censor any details you deem too sensitive. I'll tell everything my way, and if you don't like it you can rewrite it to suit your whims. Isn't that what you historians do anyway?

The reason I put myself in dangerous situations is not because I want to die. It's because I want to really live. Since I know I'll keep on breathing until I reach a ripe old, old age, my challenge is to make my life worth something.

And how can I know this, I can hear you asking.

It's because Sam won't let me die.

He's good at his job, too. He's been keeping the ruling Emperor and Crown Heir from unnatural death since the Tarkle line was founded over a thousand years ago. He's the ultimate bodyguard, our Sam.

He's also a sentient black hole, a space/time singularity. Although he says he exists outside of time, he's been my constant companion all my life. He's also been my father's all his life, too, as strange as that sounds. Now, maybe some wirehead physicist can explain how the same entity can be in two - or sometimes occasionally more - places at the same time, but all I know is that he claims things look different from his perspective. To him it is always now, whether he is with me, my great-to-the-X grandfather, or one of my yet-to-be-born descendants. There is no past or future to him, yet he can remember what we've talked about or done in my past. But when I ask if he 'remembers' what will happen to me tomorrow, he just says it doesn't work like that. I gave up trying to make sense of it a long time ago.

What's even stranger about his whole outside-of-time thing is that he always knows where to be to absorb a bullet or energy blast that's headed my way. I've asked him about that, too, and all I got was something about him being attuned to the space/time shadows of potentially fatal events.

Yeah, spooky, I know.

So yeah, I've got this microscopic pinpoint of nothingness that's always close by. And as you can tell, we can talk to each other, although we don't use sound. See, in addition to him being in control of his gravity and mass - he says these are leakages from higher dimensions that he can direct at will - he is also telepathic.

That's right, he talks to me just like psionics get in people's heads. No one around me can hear him, and they never know when I'm talking to him. It's kind of cool, really, but it would be better if he didn't have such a disapproving attitude towards gambling. I mean, how hard would it be for him to zip around and tell me what cards everyone else is holding?

But I digress. Basically, he's just there to keep me breathing. I've taken many a knock that I'm sure he could have warned me about, and that brings us back to my waking up in the alley behind the *Crooked Shaft*.

I'd set down at the spaceport serving the oldest settlement on Herrig's, a town bearing the ambitious name 'Good Luck City', shortly after local noon. My ship, the *Wah*, is, to all outward appearances, nothing special to look at and seems to be in need of so much work that even a semi-desperate thief would sneer at it and keep right on going, so I felt comfortable enough leaving it there among the other hard-luck freighters.

Both the spaceport and the town - it by no means qualified as a city, despite being nearly the only permanent habitation on the whole planet and having been there for over 300 years - were enclosed by an encircling repulsor fence that was a good 20 feet high. Seeing that made me really not want to meet any of the local beasts. Apparently the high oxygen content of the atmosphere let the natives grow to truly impressive proportions.

I'll tell you, I couldn't help but double-check the power cell in my blaster pistol. If the repulsor field on that fence ever went down things could get pretty hairy really quick.

In addition to the pistol in its low-slung holster on my right hip, I also wore my usual quick-staff - collapsed, of course - on my left. It felt good to be able to wear it, too. Whenever I have to visit one of the so-called civilized worlds and can't wear it, I feel like I'm missing an arm or something.

Anyway, for the rest of my outfit I'd chosen a blackened armored vest over a t-shirt, khaki cargo pants that had seen better days, and well-worn low-top work boots. I wanted to blend in with the local function-before-fashion mindset, giving anyone that saw me the impression I was just another scoundrel who wasn't afraid of a little hard work looking to get in on the big bucks to be made working the mines.

Or the bigger bucks to be made running ore out-system to unapproved buyers.

See, it's like this: minzite ore is so crucial to the functioning of our space-faring metaculture that one of my forward-thinking ancestor Emperors decided to tax the hell out of it. The rates are high enough when it's being sold within the empire, and truly exorbitant when anyone from outside wants any.

So while it's an accepted fact that some smuggling is unavoidable, there are all kinds of checks and regulations in place to try and keep the rate of it down to a minimum. The Imperial Trade Commission maintains an orbital facility here and has the right to board and inspect any vessel leaving the planet. Large commercial freighters are required to clear their cargo manifests with them before being given permission to depart, and smaller ships are subject to 'random' searches. To enforce their regulations the ITC maintains a squadron of starfighters and can, of course, call in the navy if necessary.

Yes, it had occurred to me that the sudden decline in reported ore production just might be related to an increase in illicit sales.

So, what was I going to do about it? Why, get in on the action myself, of course.

And where does any would-be smuggler worth his salt go to get the low-down on the local business opportunities? Where else but the to the saloons?

That's right - Herrig's World is so much like the Old West of ancient Earth in the minds of its inhabitants that the bars-slash-casinos are called saloons here. They might not have bat-wing doors opening off a raised wooden boardwalk, and there aren't brass spittoons surrounded by stinking globs of tobacco spit, but I'd bet if someone zapped a gunslinger from old Dodge City to here, he'd feel right at home.

I know I certainly did. I made for one of the larger ones.

The early-afternoon clientele - I hesitate to use the word 'crowd' to describe at most 20 patrons in a place that could easily hold ten times that many - of the *Crooked Shaft* was mainly men who had the look of unemployed-but-hopeful potential miners. There were a couple of women included in this mix, too, once I took a better look around; ladies they would never be called. The real 'working ladies' would show up about the same time the miner's work shift ended, I was sure. And then there were the three or four - one I couldn't be sure of - professional gamblers that were inevitably attracted to places like Herrig's that offered good pay to not-so-good men.

They were just who I was looking for.

My first stop was at the bar, of course, since everyone knows that a newcomer who doesn't check in with the bartender first has no business being in a place like this. It still being rather early, I asked for a cup of coffee. The price was, as expected, quite high, but I didn't quibble. I certainly didn't want to come off as a guy who couldn't afford to spend a few credits.

The man behind the bar looked like he might have been a minzite miner in his day. Of medium height and stocky build, his scar-covered bald head and bloodshot eyes told a tale of a hard life that was only accented further by the cybernetic right arm with which he handed me my coffee. He sounded friendly enough, though, when he asked me if I was new to Herrig's.

I couldn't deny it, not that I wanted to. "That's right. Just set down today, in fact," I told him.

He looked me up and down with the appraising eye of someone who knows what to look for. After a few moments of this silent scrutiny he told me, "You might just have it in you to make a go of it here."

I thanked him, not sure what I might have said if I hadn't measured up to his standards.

((He looked you over with more than his eyes,)) Sam said directly into my brain. ((That arm of his has some sort of active scanner in it. I cannot tell how many of your implants he picked up.))

That's something else about Sam. He can see in just about every range of the electromagnetic spectrum. A radio transmitting shines like a light panel to him. Now, he's not a computer. He can seldom decode the signals that he sees, but he always knows they're there. And sometimes knowing is half the battle, as some philosopher once said.

(Whether he did or not, I can't see it making much of a difference in how much he charges me for a drink,) I replied silently. I like to throw non-sequiturs like that at him every once in a while, just for the fun of it.

"So, you'll be looking for work, then?" the barkeep asked.

I nodded. "But maybe something that pays a little better than busting rock. I've got my own ship and she'll carry more than you'd think, if you get my drift."

In the timeless tradition of bartenders everywhere he swiped a damp rag across the bar as he looked around to see if anyone was paying us any attention. He must have been satisfied because after a few seconds he said, "You know you could lose that ship of yours if you get caught carrying ore." It wasn't a question. "But if you're determined to try and make a run anyway, I hear there may be certain individuals around town who have been known to set up shippers with clients that prefer to remain a discreet distance removed from us here."

Jackpot! And on my first pull of the handle, as it were.

"Now that might be information a man could use. Yes indeed."

I sipped my coffee, leaning against the bar like I had all the time in the galaxy. Undue haste in these types of dealings is often a sign to one party or the other that something is not on the level.

While I waited for him to make the next move, one of the hopeful miners came up and ordered a pitcher of beer for him and his companions, who were seated around a table playing cards. With my practiced eye I saw it was a low-stakes game, which explained why none of the professional gamblers were involved.

When the man had departed with his beer, the barkeep explained that his usual afternoon waitress had unexpectedly quit on him yesterday and he hadn't found a replacement yet. "I heard she left with this fellow she'd taken up with whose contract was up. For some reason, he couldn't get off-world fast enough. So now, here I am short-handed again. I tell you, friend, there just ain't enough women on this rock."

"I can't imagine why not."

"Hmph. Anyway, about what I was saying. You think you might be interested?"

Upholding another age-old custom, he cast a meaningful glance toward his tip jar, which held mostly single-credit coins and a few fives.

Taking the hint, I casually reached into the inside pocket of my vest. (Is anyone watching?) I asked Sam.

((One of the female miners keeps glancing your way, but she is occupied at the moment. Other than her, no one has shown any undue interest in you.))

Selecting four 20's by feel, I quietly slid them onto the bar under my hand. As soon as I withdrew, the coins vanished into his rag. A timeless classic never grows old.

The barest hint of a smile made a brief foray onto his face before running back into hiding. "As it so happens, one of the fellows we were discussing usually puts in an appearance here most evenings, say from 7 to 9 or thereabouts. If you were to be here then, it would be my pleasure to put in a good word on your behalf."

To a true player, the game is everything. "Well now, that would be mighty kind of you. I'd be much obliged."

"Nothing to it. All part of keeping my customers satisfied."

So, business taken care of, I saw no reason not to relax and enjoy myself. Seeing as how there was an empty seat at the table with the two gamblers and three miners, I sauntered over and got myself invited to sit in. Poker was the game, and for the next few hours I gave and took in about equal amounts while the bar grew quite crowded and significantly noisier, until at last I decided I'd waited long enough.

Since I had enjoyed the laid-back low-pressure way our games had been played, I arranged for one of the hopeful miners to win a sizeable pot from me, then used that as my excuse to withdraw. "It's been thoroughly enjoyable, gentlemen, but my stomach is getting far too familiar with my backbone," I told them, and that was that. I usually gamble because I enjoy the companionship, not out of any desire to win a huge fortune. Something to do with growing up rich, I suppose.

The place was quite rowdy by this point, which didn't surprise me at all. In fact, if it hadn't gotten a little energetic I would have wondered what was wrong. The one place that was an island of calm was in the immediate vicinity of a particular corner table. It came as no shock to me when my bartender friend pointed out the man holding court there was the one I needed to talk to. He had already mentioned me to him, he said, so I casually worked my way to the periphery of his domain.

Foral Tenew, the man's name was. Expensively dressed in some fashion designer's idea of show-the-wealth and a shipload of flashy jewelry, he was a tall, slender guy with too-perfect facial features and a flawless olive complexion. Everything about him screamed new money makeover. I started to wonder if I was already on the verge of cracking the whole missing-minzite mystery wide open on my first day there.

Turns out I was wrong.

He was seated between a gorgeous redhead in a nearly transparent sheath of a dress and a pair of bio-augmented toughs. He and the redhead

had glasses of some no-doubt pricey concoction before them, while the muscle boys sipped draft beers.

Seeing me approach, he whispered in the redhead's ear and she got up and left in the direction of the bar. I wasn't supposed to hear him say, "Keep an eye on this one but give us some space," but that's what my hearing augment is for.

"Why don't you join us, my man?" he said in a friendly enough manner. I got the distinct impression that his tone - indeed, his whole demeanor - was a practiced act. What it concealed I didn't know yet, but even that first line was enough to make me wary.

"Arll tells me you're a freighter pilot," he said after I'd slid in beside him. "And that you might be looking to pick up a cargo."

I distinctly didn't like this guy; there was just something that screamed 'sleazeball' in his every action. Still, he was the only lead I had at the time so I swallowed my bile and acted nice. It was either deal with him or go back to the spaceport and start asking the other pilots where they were going and who they were selling to. At least with Tenew I stood a slight chance of not being lied to or shot outright.

"That's right. And he tells me you're the man who can hook me up with the best buyers."

"Yeah, good ol' Arll. So tell me a little about yourself, Mr. Pilot. How do I know you can get my merchandise where it needs to go?"

"Well, for starters the name is Jed Ecnirp." I didn't offer to shake hands. For one thing, I wasn't sure I trusted myself not to crush his into a bloody pulp. He just had that effect on me, and I didn't even know him yet. Sometimes I wonder if I'm a little bit psychic.

And yes, I used my standard pseudonym. You'd be surprised how few people ever catch on to the joke.

Anyway, I went on to tell him that I'd been running shady for a dozen years and hadn't been caught yet. I informed him that there is considerably more cargo space in my ship than is apparent and that its engines are well above average for a vessel in its class. In other words, feeding him exactly what he wanted to hear. And none of it was untrue, either. I just didn't tell him how I'd come upon such a special ship or just how special it really is.

I also hinted that I was not above employing certain illegal defenses if the situation ever became desperate enough, which earned me a toothy smile. This was just further confirmation of his character, as if I needed it.

Which I certainly didn't, not after what he said next.

"Good, good. I like what I'm hearing, Mr. Ecnirp. Now tell me a little about yourself. I didn't get to where I am now -" He waved his hands to point at, I presume, his clothes and jewelry. "- by placing blind trust in just everyone. No, sir. There are too many people in this galaxy who will say anything, promise anything, then cut and run the first time things get a little sticky. Oh, I'm not saying you're like that -" he gave a humorless laugh and false smile. "- but maybe you are. I just don't know yet.

"So here's the deal," he said, shifting to a harder, more business-like tone. "Anyone who works for me has to prove he's got what it takes before I'll trust him with my merchandise."

I didn't like the direction in which this interview was turning, but what could I do? Some kind of test was always possible in this kind of operation, and it's not like I'm overly squeamish. "And how would I do that, Mr. Tenew?"

There was that cold, predatory smile again. "As it just so happens, the mining company I am affiliated with is getting ready to move one of its work towns. And lucky for you, their clearing crew is moving out tomorrow morning. You'll go with them, and if you survive I'll know you've got what it takes to work for me. Deal?"

What choice did I have? I needed to know who he's selling to, and the only way I was going to find that out was to go to work for him. I agreed to his terms but did so in a way that made it clear that if he didn't have a haulage job for me on his return, I would be very unhappy with him. "Alright, if that's how it's got to be. But let me tell you something: I'm a hard man to kill. When I get back I expect you to honor your word as well. Cross me and you'll need a lot more protection than Bo and Luke here."

The sneer on his face said what he thought my chances against his bio-augments were, but the slight tremor in his voice told me he wasn't 100% convinced of his safety nonetheless. "Now, now, there's no need for threats, Mr. Ecnirp. Demonstrate your loyalty to me and I'll reward your service. I'm a man of my word."

"Good. I'll be seeing you."

As I got up and left, I didn't need Sam to tell me his two bodyguards were sizing me up. I'm sure they thought they could take me. After all, I'm just an average-sized man and they were bulging with augmented muscles and full of all sorts of internal enhancements. But what they didn't know is that I have some enhancements of my own. I just don't want any of mine to show. The element of surprise can be worth a lot in a fight.

△△△

I didn't have to ask what a clearing crew is because I'd heard all about them from the men I played cards with earlier. As hard and tough as they tried to appear, and as badly as they wanted work, not one of them was desperate enough to sign on with that company. Clearing a new site in preparation for one of the mobile towns to come in is considered the most dangerous job on the whole planet, and with good reason.

All the wildlife in the selected area had to be driven out before the repulsor fence could be erected, and according to the Indigenous Life Protection Act - an Imperial decree wrangled by some bleeding-heart lobbyist group centuries ago - every effort had to be made to do so without harming the native creatures. Never mind that the creatures in question are so strong and well-armed that armored vehicles are to them merely soft wrappers containing delicious food. They are the ones who need protecting from us vicious, bloodthirsty humans.

And since the best way for us to stay alive is to take advantage of our small size and nimble ability to hide among the ceramic foliage, we got to go in there on our own two feet.

Needless to say, there weren't too many volunteers for the job. One of the gamblers had even warned me not to be anywhere near the east end of the spaceport field in the morning or else I might get 'invited' to join the departing crew. When he said that I had thought it sounded like a very sensible idea to be elsewhere then. Now here I was planning on going there on purpose. Sometimes my life is just one fun adventure after another.

With my business in the bar concluded at last and having had nothing more than beer and a plate of nachos while I gambled the afternoon away, my stomach begged attention. I decided that I owed myself a better dinner than the Crooked Shaft could offer, especially considering the new job I was setting out on tomorrow, so I began working my way through the boisterous crowd toward the door.

Now, normally I prefer not to spend evenings alone, and almost certainly not after a long flight. On Herrig's World, though, I was ready to make an exception. The 'professional' ladies available at the bar all seemed to be too used-up for my taste, and there didn't appear to be any other options. Even the miner chick that had been eyeing me earlier was nowhere to be seen, so I was all prepared to go it stag when I beheld such a vision of feminine perfection that my breath caught in my throat and my heart skipped a beat.

And no, I'm not making this up. That really happened. My neuroware even logged it to my medical profile.

Hair the color of burnished bronze floated in playful curls around a face that a Greek goddess would have killed for. Lustrous emerald eyes twinkled amongst prominent but not over-large cheekbones, an adorable button nose and a sensual mouth with lips that had to have been made for kissing.

A pale blue and silver dress hung off one dainty shoulder and was cut to give her ample cleavage magnificent exposure before descending via her flat stomach and slightly flared hips to end in a knee-length pleated skirt. Even her toes, seen at the tips of her sparkly sandals, were perfectly shaped and adorned by glossy blue polish on their nails. She couldn't have been more than 25 standard, and the top of her head only came up to my chin.

I was smitten, no doubt about it.

When I saw her she was standing alone just inside the door, looking over the crowd as if she knew she could have her pick of any man there. I almost felt sorry for them, for I knew they didn't stand a chance; not once I set my sights on her.

"They are all unworthy of a goddess such as you," I said softly, hang taken a position beside her as if it were my right to do so.

She turned those intoxicating green eyes upon me, flicking them quickly down and back up. "Is that so?" she replied, her voice a warm, sensual caress upon my ears.

"Indeed. For how could any of us lowly mortals ever hope to join you, who shines with the radiance of the heavens?"

"Is there not one here who might aspire to forestall my loneliness, then?" She pouted and my heart melted. And her words, they set my soul alight. I could listen to her melodious utterances forever.

"There is one, unworthy though I may be."

"And who is this one who presumes to be of more worth than these other poor wretches?"

Oh, her every word was honey to a man starved for any sweetness. I offered her a sweeping bow and said, "None other than your humble subject Jed Ecnirp, your grace. And may I beg to know by what divine appellation I may address you?"

Her smile could brighten a faded sun. "I'm Nicolette."

Nicole-ette. Such a doubly feminine name was an absolutely perfect fit for this amazing woman. I could not imagine any moniker more appropriate.

"Nicolette," I said, luxuriating in the feel of it on my tongue. "I have longed to meet you my entire life, yet I knew it not until this moment. Please, would you care to join me for a drink? Or dinner? Or a life of extravagance in the Glittering Palace on Alphum?"

That heart-warming smile continued to radiate its life-giving essence on me. "Perhaps a drink first. Then we can talk about where to go from there."

I could see my entire future opening up before me from that moment on. We would fall madly in love, and when I finally revealed to her that my offer of the palace was for real, she would gladly consent to be my queen. It was all falling into place so perfectly.

That, of course, is when everything went horribly wrong.

One moment I was offering the love of my life my arm to escort her to a table, the next I heard some kind of commotion behind us and Sam was warning me to duck, now!

The crackle of a blaster bolt ionizing the air where your head was a second before has a way of engraving itself in your memory. This one sounded just like the others I've heard, yet there was a big difference. This time I had someone else besides myself to worry about.

Relieved beyond measure to find her unharmed, I pulled Nicolette to me and began working us toward the door. I had to get her to safety before I could deal with whatever was happening behind me.

I was so preoccupied with this that I never even sensed the blow coming that knocked me out.

CHAPTER 2

(W)hat the nova happened?) I asked Sam. I sat up carefully, taking inventory of the rest of my body, but found no other injuries. Unfortunately, I couldn't say the same for my possessions. I had neither blaster, armor vest, nor money. The only reason whoever rolled me didn't take my customized quick-staff was that they couldn't defeat the security feature that keeps it firmly attached to my forearm or hip unless my neuroware releases it. I'm glad they couldn't, too. Unlike the other items, I didn't have a replacement for it aboard the *Wah*.

((You were hit on the back of your head with a beer bottle, then carried out and around the saloon and deposited here.))

(Yeah, I got that part.) I saw that it was still dark, so I hadn't been out all night. (How long ago?)

((Approximately eight hours. It is now approaching 05:30 local time. Dawn is due in roughly 45 minutes.))

I was confused for a moment until I remembered from my research that the day here is only 22.5 standard hours long. At least I hadn't missed the departure of the clearing crew. I stood up slowly, and after depositing the beer I'd drunk for recycling, made for the street. (Why so long?)

((Your attacker, whether by luck or intent, hit the base of your skull directly over your neural implant's processor core. I presume the shock to it overloaded your system and it took that long for the implant to repair itself and activate your healing nanites.))

That was a sobering thought. As far as I knew, only one person had scanned me for implants, and he was known to be for sale. But why would he sell me out? I filed the question away for later. There were more important things to deal with first. (And what happened to Nicolette?)

((I do not know. Once you went down she fled out the front door.))

Something about that didn't sound right. (Alone?)

((Several other patrons were leaving as well, but she did not appear to be having anything to do with any of them.))

That didn't make any sense. Why had she abandoned me? Something fishy was going on, I just knew it. The problem was, I couldn't afford to hang around long enough to figure out what it was, not unless I wanted to blow my one shot at infiltrating the smuggling ring. Because one thing was for certain: if I walked out on my agreement with Tenew, I'd never be given another chance with any of the other bosses.

The city streets this time of morning weren't practically deserted, they were absolutely, completely deserted. I encountered not a single soul on my jog from the bar back to the space-port and the *Wah*. And trust me, I wish I had. Then I might have been able to get a ride. Even with the accelerated healing my implants grant me, jogging any distance after being hit in the head with a thick glass beer bottle was not my idea of fun.

As I went, every step jarring my brain a little looser, I asked Sam why he hadn't prevented that attack like he had with the blaster shot. I should have known better than to bother asking, but having a reason to rail at him took my mind off my pain.

((As you know, when I can prevent a non-life threatening injury to you without revealing my presence I will do so. In this situation, since I foresaw assault would be non-fatal, I chose not to intervene. I was not going to make my presence known by acting overtly. I'm sorry you got hit, but you will recover.))

I let him have it for the whole way back to the ship. He deserved it, and it made me feel a little bit better.

ΔΔΔ

Once inside, the first thing I did was grab a couple of fullmeal bars and wolf them down. I had missed a couple of meals by then and my stomach let me know who the real boss was.

I figured I just had time to change clothes, re-arm myself and pack a backpack before I'd have to hightail it to meet up with my new work detail, and I was right. They hadn't started boarding the transport yet, but it was a close call.

There were about 20 of the hardest, meanest-looking men I've ever seen milling about near the only vehicle on the eastern airfield, so I knew I'd found the crew. By the time I jogged over to them one had separated himself from the others and stood waiting for me. By his stern look and crisp, rigid body language I pegged him as ex-military. He was tall, broad and crewcut, wearing the snagless jungle suit favored by adventurers and soldiers the galaxy over.

"So you must be the yahoo Mr. Tenew was going on about," he growled. I'm sure if he'd had the chewed-up nub of a cigar in his mouth he would have spit it out and ground it under his boot.

"Looky here, boys," he said, much louder. "This here hotshot is the feller who's supposed to be able to out-shoot, out-fly, and out-hump any three of us. He don't look like all that to me, but the boss says he's the best of the best, and the boss is always right."

I couldn't believe it. That slimy, Arcturian spiketoad-licking, worm-slurping, bottom-feeder had managed to set every single one of the toughest men on the planet against me before I even met them. Never mind that what he'd said about me was all true. He couldn't have known that. Now, instead of being able to slip in as one of the crew, I was going to have to prove myself against every man there.

It started immediately.

"He shore don't look too tough t' me!" shouted someone in the middle of the pack.

"Who's he think he is?" another asked, followed by, "Don't nobody say dey can out-shoot ol' Gus."

"I'm gonna teach him to come talkin' trash 'round me," said yet another. The taunts and threats kept coming. All the while I just stood there and kept my mouth shut, letting them get their first reactions out of their systems.

After a few minutes the leader silenced them with a shouted, "Enough!" Then he turned back to me and demanded to know what I had to say for myself.

I knew I had only one chance to get off to the right start with guys like these. "Against any other group of bozos I always stand out as the one to beat, but I'm sure each of you knows that feeling. Looks like I finally found my equals."

There. Men like that can't stand for anyone to think he's better than them, but they'll gladly welcome another who is up to their level of competence. Provided that he isn't all talk, that is.

"We'll see about that," came the challenge I'd fully expected to hear.

The crowd parted as a tall, lean whip of a man stepped forward, collapsed quick-staff in hand. He pointed it toward my own. "Didn't nobody never tell you not to carry a weapon you ain't ready to use?"

I darted my eyes to the commander, paying him the respect of asking permission. His slight nod was all I needed to see.

My staff was out, fully extended and swinging toward Slim's right knee before he could even flick his own weapon to full length, much less block with it. Only a reflexive step backward kept him on his feet. After that it was on for real. He was good, I'll give him that. But I'm better.

We whirled and blocked, jumped and wove, spun and danced. He never got a hit through. After I tapped his armor vest a few times and he still kept coming, I decided I'd have to up the ante. I blocked a couple more of his attacks, then, using a move I learned in my time spent training under one of the galaxy's foremost staff masters, I slid the tip of my weapon between his hands and disarmed him with a twist and a yank. I then, on the reverse, brought the end of my staff to a dead stop less than an inch from the back of his neck.

He knew he would have been dead had that blow connected. Everyone else knew it, too.

"Hey, Pete! What happened?"

"Damn, man, that dude's fast!"

"Did you see that?"

Once again the men sounded off, but this time most of their cries were in my favor. After a minute or two of this their leader stepped up to me, drew himself up in a crisp military posture, and extended his right hand. "I'm Sergeant Jesk Fowler. Welcome to the Devil's Rejects."

△△△

"So this is how it works," the sergeant told me and the two other virgins a short time later, as we flew toward our target. "We start by dropping a screamer in the middle of the zone. That'll get most of the critters moving out. Problem is, the biggest and baddest ain't gonna run from any little noisemaker."

"So that's where we come in, is it?" I asked.

"You catch on quick. What we gotta do fer 'em is herd 'em outta the zone using our bangers." He showed us a weapon that looked like a cross between an ancient Tommy-gun and a sawed-off shotgun, if you can imagine one that fired slugs almost an inch in diameter from an 18-inch long barrel. It was fed from a drum magazine the length of the barrel and about 12 inches across that reminded me of a pony keg of beer.

"This baby's rounds don't penetrate, but they really ring their bells. What we do is, two or three of us stand around in the directions we don't want them to go and pop a few at them. These big dinos ain't all that stupid, so they usually figure there's one direction they can go that don't hurt."

"And that's all there is to it?" one of the other new recruits asked. "Sounds like a piece of cake. If I'd knowed it was that easy I'd of signed on a year ago instead of busting my balls dragging a vapor-vac hose around all day down in some hole in the ground."

One of the veterans sneered and told him, "Oh, yeah, it's a cake walk alright, right up to the point when you realize that a whole pack of raptors wants to thank you for delivering dinner. Do you know how they'll express their gratitude? By eating you first!"

That brought a round of boisterous laughter from the rest of the Rejects and a look of shock from the newbie.

"Whaddya' mean, raptors? Sarge just said them screamers would run off..."

"I said 'most critters', like the big plant eaters. The 'big and bads' are big, solitary hunters like old T-Rex, and bangers usually work for them. And then there are the raptors. Raptors are in a class all by themselves. They're what you might call the apex predators on this rock. Pack hunters, agile for their size, and pretty slick and cunning."

"So why... why didn't you say nothing 'bout them?"

The sergeant drilled him with a look that could have withered a Jeftlian stone tree. "Maybe because I was interrupted by a smartass know-it-all before I got to them yet. What was your name again?"

"It's... it's Perkins, sir. Rondy Perkins."

"No, it ain't. Your name is Raptorbait. You got a problem with that, Raptorbait?"

"No, sir. Raptorbait it is."

"Good. Now, as I was saying, the only problem with using bangers to herd the big guys is that sometimes they figure out there's another way to stop the hurt. If there ain't too much overhead cover, that's a good time to use your jump packs. You can also make for the heart of an irontree cluster and keep popping bangers at him if there's one nearby.

"Or if, and I stress only if, you have no other way to evade an imminent attack on your person are you authorized to use deadly force. Remember, the ILPA was passed for a reason, and we are legally required to abide by it."

In a tone that had the tang of long tradition behind it, one of the Rejects in the back of the transport asked, "And why was it passed, Sarge?"

"Because a million years from now his descendants might just become sentient," came the ritual response.

"And why do we care?" was the second half of the traditional question.

"Because Big Brother is watching!" everyone chorused, completing the ritual.

All this told me one thing: these guys couldn't care less about the actual reason for a law that protected predatory creatures who thought they were crunchy and would taste good with or without ketchup. The legally-mandated compliance monitors built into certain key pieces of equipment, on the other hand, could tag a violator and lead to him getting slapped with a seriously heavy fine or even prison time. When an Emperor passes a law, he intends for it to be followed.

"But what do we do about the raptors?" Raptorbait asked.

"Well, for them the law's a little different. They fall under the heading of 'incorrigibly hostile', so the self-preservation clause kicks in. The only good raptor is a dead raptor. Right, gentlemen?"

Raptorbait kept the rest of his questions to himself after that, so the rest of the briefing went a lot faster. Basically, I learned that after we cleared an area, the size of which depended on how thick the vegetation was, we would all take positions on its perimeter and the hovering transport would unleash the hellish energies of its disruptor beams and vaporize everything down to the dirt. Once this sequence was repeated often enough, we would drop a portable generator and set up a repulsor fence around the site. And voila! suddenly there would be a safe zone for a mobile town to be dropped into.

It all sounded so easy, talking about it way up above the jungle canopy. But as I well know, life is never as rosy as it looks from a distance.

About the only thing that wasn't a whole lot worse than advertised was the jungle itself. As I said before, a lot of the native creatures get really, really, big here. I'm talking on the order of Earth's dinosaurs on growth hormones. But unlike on the homeworld, trees aren't allowed to grow too close to one another. It's like the biggest critters demand room to walk between them. So you end up with a tight cluster of really tall, ceramic-reinforced stalks - all one plant, really - that shoot straight up some fifty feet or more before branching out into a dense tangle that forms a ceiling that comes near to blocking out the sunlight.

And sure, there's some underbrush. The worst of it is something the guys call 'pokey-bush'. Think briar thickets with foot-long, super-hard needles for thorns. That stuff is a mess you do not want to come down in the middle of.

△△△

The first day I came close to feeding at least three different dinos. Now, everyone called them dinos, but I don't want you thinking these were anywhere near as tame as anything Earth ever evolved. Most every species is encased in ceramic armor that ranges from scales to plates to full-blown shells. This stuff isn't terribly light either, so nature here came up with some really strong and efficient muscle tissue. These beasts are big, hard, and strong. And that's just for starters. The herbivore equivalent here has jaws that could crush granite, while the ones that prey on them are just downright nasty. Their arsenal includes wrecking balls, battering rams, supersonic whips, oscillating saws and vibrating spikes operating at incredibly high frequencies, among other things.

The one redeeming quality they all have in common, though, is that none of them are what we would call speed demons. Oh, don't get me wrong, they're fast enough when they get moving in a straight line. What I'm talking about is more their reaction speeds. A nimble man can move a lot faster than even most of the predators can deal with. A feint and a duck and roll to the side is usually enough to get you out of most situations.

That is, unless it involves raptors. Once again, they're in a class by themselves. Built on the standard quadruped body plan, their highest point is the front shoulder, which is about 7 feet off the ground. This is because they have terribly awesome long front legs, jam-packed with the super-strong Herrig's World muscles, that terminate in slightly curved triple talons a foot long that are designed to slide in between armor plates and rip them off their prey. To the rear, their bodies slope down to thick legs equally adept at running and jumping, and on which they can stand upright and sort-of walk, although not very fast or gracefully. And in front of all this is a huge head on a long, thick neck with a pair of forward-looking predator's eyes above a snout ending in a leech-like round mouth equipped with a double ring of razor-sharp boring teeth. It likes to shove this into the holes it rips in its victim's armor and take deep, debilitating bites.

And, as Sarge told us, these puppies are fast and smart. So much so that I nearly had one of those deep, debilitating bites taken out of me despite my best efforts.

It was still fairly early in the morning, and I and two other Rejects were using our bangers to try to persuade a medium-sized ambush hunter that it was time to get up and go find somewhere else to wait for breakfast. We weren't having much success in getting him to abandon the pokey-bush patch he was hiding in, though, since most of our banger rounds got deflected before they reached him.

When he finally did get up and those extra-long legs of his started carrying him over the top of the thicket I thought, in my inexperience, that one of us had finally managed to land a couple of rounds on a sensitive spot

Silly me. I should have known better.

I also should have been paying more attention to what was behind me.

The first I knew of trouble was when I heard a blaster go off somewhere to my right around the edge of the thicket. What with ceramics being so heavy there aren't any flying creatures that need shooting, so that left only one thing my partner could have been gunning for. And where there's one, there's a bunch.

I turned around just in time to see one charging straight towards me from not more than 20 yards away. Now, I've been in many situations where I've found myself staring head-on into danger, and I've never yet had to go change my underwear because of it. But if there had ever been anything that got me closer to dropping a load than that raptor bearing down on me, I've mercifully forgotten it.

I'm not the type to freeze up in a surprise encounter with danger, either. That's not a viable survival trait. But no matter how fast my reflexes are, I've no doubt I'd be dead if not for Sam's intervention. There was just not time for me to drop my banger, draw and fire my blaster, and get out of the way of that mountain of armor-scaled flesh.

It was no more than 3 yards from me and closing when it suddenly collapsed in on itself, vanishing into nothing in a split-second implosion with nothing more than a dull pop of air rushing in to fill the void left by its exit from this universe.

Seeing Sam devour something never fails to remind me just how awesomely powerful he really is. If it wasn't for his ability to shunt his huge mass and its inherent space-time distortion more commonly known as gravity off into another dimension, he would suck in everything around him. People, ships, asteroids, planets, stars - anything and everything is fair fodder for an unshielded black hole.

(Thanks. That was close.)

((Lucky for you neither of your teammates are nearby.))

(Yeah, otherwise you would have had to let me get eaten.)

((Never. There might have been a reason to arrange for the witnesses to be, however.))

One thing about Sam: he doesn't have much of a sense of humor. He meant what he said. He takes the idea of keeping his existence a secret very seriously.

Fortunately for all of us, the rest of the raptor pack chose to pursue the fleeing mountain of meat instead of hanging around with us merely snack-sized morsels.

The other two times I almost fed a dino that first day I was able to pull my own fat out of the fire. Once, a T-Rex type decided to try and snatch me up on his way by, but a jump-pack assisted hop kept me from becoming fast food. And later, it was my nimble ducking and weaving that kept me out of the jaws of a giant crocodile-sort until a sustained volley of bangers fired by no less than four rejects convinced him to move on.

The only plus to all the excitement was that it kept me from thinking about Nicolette. Constantly trying to make sense of her abandoning me was driving me nuts. Thoughts of her even superseded my wonderings about who shot at me and why.

To say that I was dead tired that evening would not even come close to how exhausted I felt. It might have had something to do with spending the previous night sprawled unconscious across bags of trash and a cold alley, but I'm just guessing.

So was I allowed to simply crawl back into my bunk aboard the transport and crash until morning like a good little trooper? Of course not.

It seems there is a tradition among the Devil's Rejects of officially welcoming in any newbie who survives his first day in the field. I won't go into details, save to say that the raptor bait, Vaughn, and I each consumed a large quantity of alcohol on the insistence of each and every veteran.

△△△

Hangover pills can be a real lifesaver. I don't even want to think what that second day would have been like if I'd gone out into the jungle half as drunk as I was when I woke up.

I lived through it, that's about the best that can be said about the day. There was a lot of running involved and I drained two jump pack power cells, all because a herd of a dozen huge plant-eaters chose to ignore our screamers.

And I thought I'd been tired the first day.

One of the last things I remember before passing out on my bunk that night was promising myself I'd install more exercise equipment in the *Wah*, and maybe make myself use it. My endurance was way down.

I survived the third day in the field, too. Unfortunately, the same cannot be said about Raptorbait.

He was working with a group of veterans some distance from where I was, so I didn't see it happen, but you can bet we all heard about it that night. And yes, it was, ironically enough, a raptor that got him.

Before we headed back to Good Luck City at the end of our 8-day job, two other men were dead as well. One fell victim to an enraged dino that refused to leave her nest full of eggs and the other was stung to death by a swarm of something like flying insects.

They said it was an average deployment, casualty wise. When I was asked if I would go out with them next time, I said I'd think about it if I hadn't had another job offer by then. These were the kind of guys it was definitely better to remain on friendly terms with.

It being early evening when we disembarked from the transport, I stopped by the *Wah* only long enough to drop off my equipment, clean up, and change back into my town clothes before heading out to the *Crooked Shaft*. I had more than one overdue business matter to attend to.

CHAPTER 3

Mr. Tenew wasn't there yet, so I confronted Arll the bartender first.

"I need to know exactly what happened the last time I was in here."

The bar was neither deserted nor especially quiet, but I was in no mood to care. Arll must have seen something of that in the set of my eyes, for he didn't even try to deflect me. After signaling for the other bartender to cover for him he told me to follow him to the back.

His office was a cramped affair, made more so by the fact that it serves double-duty as overflow stockroom. Cases of imported liquors were stacked to the ceiling, leaving just enough room for him to get to his paper-strewn desk. It had a door, though, which cut the noise down to an acceptable level as well as ensure our privacy.

He took a seat in the only chair and pointed to a corner of his desk for me. "Do you know who the woman you were talking to is?"

I don't know what I was expecting him to say, but that sure wasn't it. This conversation promised to get real interesting real fast. "She said her name was Nicolette."

He nodded his scarred head. "It is. Nicolette Tar-Nevin."

I was starting to get a tingle in my scalp, which often happens when I'm on the track of something big. "As in Tar-Nevin Mining?"

He nodded his head. "You were chatting up the owner's daughter."

Talk about going straight to the top. Tar-Nevin Mining is the biggest and oldest of the locally owned companies, going back nearly 400 years to shortly after Herrig's World was first discovered.

"So does everyone who talks to her get shot at?"

"A few have. Her father is not thrilled about her hobnobbing with the working class."

Like there was anyone else for her to socialize with on this backwater rim world. "So it was one of her father's men who tried to zap me?"

"I didn't say that." His cybernetic arm came up to massage his bare head.

"I'm waiting," I told him, drumming the fingers of my right hand on my quick-staff suggestively.

"As near as I can tell, the shooting was an accident. Seems a drunk miner drew his blaster and started waving it around and when somebody else was trying to wrestle it away from him it went off."

"An accident, huh?" You might say I wasn't 100% convinced. "In my experience, 'accidents' usually turn out to have had some planning behind them."

He let out a nervous chuckle. "Yeah, I know what you mean. And I didn't see it happen, you understand, but I'm thinking this really could be one of those rare, true accidents. The cowboy with the gun has never had anything to do with old man Weber - that's Nicolette's father - as far as I know. And he had just lost most of his pay, from what I hear."

All right, I'm willing to admit that sometimes an accident doesn't have to actually have anything to do with me. It's unusual, but it can happen. But that still didn't account for what happened next. "And after that?"

Arll's mech-tech arm hadn't stopped rubbing his head, and he was having trouble looking at me. Now, in my travels I've seen more obvious signs of nervousness, but not very often. This guy was really worried that I wasn't going to like what he had to say next but was too smart to try to lie about it.

I thought he was going to tell me that it was Nicolette's father's goons who had clubbed me and dumped me out back. I was already considering the idea that I might have to make an end run around the whole protective-father situation to be able to see her again. I've never revealed my true identity to a woman just to get her to go out with me - I'm not like that at all - but if it was the only way I could get her father to call off his hounds, she was worth it.

So I thought Arll's hesitation was because he was waiting for me to ask how the thug knew to hit me precisely where he did.

Then he went and threw me a loop I didn't see coming at all. He said, "In the confusion, Mr. Tenew's bodyguards hit you from behind."

△△△

Those same bio-augments were once again sitting with Mr. Tenew when I approached his table. The voluptuous redhead was there as well, dressed this time in a form-fitting bodysuit that displayed an animated rainbow-hued ripple effect that was almost mesmerizing to watch. They had been joined by another flamboyantly attired man this time, and he and Tenew were chatting in hushed tones that quickly came to a halt when they saw me.

He looked me up and down and raised an eyebrow at me. "Ah, Mr. Ecnirp. How wonderful to see you again."

I stood a yard or so from the table and shot him a glaringly scathing look. "Save it. I'll deal with you in a minute. But first, I have business with the ball-less buffoons who ambushed me the other night."

Tenew's mien of friendliness evaporated faster than water in an open airlock, and the two bruisers shot to their feet. One of them started to say something, but Tenew cut him off with a savage glare before turning his serpentine gaze back to me. "Your business is with me. Anything my employees may have done is for me to deal with, not you."

My eyes never left the bodyguards, even though I spoke to Tenew. "I don't see it that way. In my book, every man is responsible for his own actions. Nobody gets off on the old 'I was just following orders' routine. If a man chooses to obey someone else, even though he knows what he's doing isn't right, that's on him and not his master."

I'll give them credit. Both bio-augs knew what was coming next, even if their boss didn't. He was still trying to argue with me even as they started to separate and assume combat postures.

Now, I do believe there are times for so-called honorable combat where everyone plays nice and no one tries to win by, say, resorting to heavy weaponry when his opponent is unarmed. I really do believe there is a place and time for that. This was neither one of those times or places.

Both of my opponents were armed with blasters and were wired to the gills with all manner of augmentations besides. They were fast, too.

But I'm faster.

My quick-staff was a blur of motion. Its first target was the gun hand of the one on my left, which shattered with a loud crunch. This shouldn't have been possible, for his bones were all carbon-fiber reinforced - that's one of the most basic enhancements these combat types go for. But, then again, my staff isn't exactly unenhanced either. In a similar manner to the way Sam can shut his mass off into another dimension, my staff can, for a few seconds at a time, substantially increase the apparent mass of its end caps. So instead of the force generated by a couple of pounds being swung at such speed, it struck with that of a hundred pounds at speed.

His hand, and the hip behind it, didn't stand a chance.

His partner actually had time to draw his blaster. I didn't know if he was going to shoot me or not, but I always assume the worst when someone pulls a weapon on me. Call it a character flaw if you want, but I don't like being shot at. I shattered his forearm on my upswing, then for good measure took out one of his knees. I hadn't forgotten waking up in a garbage heap, and I wasn't in a particularly forgiving mood.

A sharp look was all it took to get rid of Tenew's companion. When he was gone I collapsed my staff and let it attach to my left forearm, then got both bodyguards' blasters and set them in the middle of the table before taking the vacated seat.

I deliberately turned my back on the two goons on the floor (Let me know if either of them goes for a weapon,) I told Sam, although I'm sure I didn't have to.

"Now then," I said with a smile false enough to rival one of Tenew's own. "I believe you and I have a flight schedule to discuss."

He was sputtering mad. "You had no right to…"

"Didn't I?" I stopped him cold.

"How did you… I paid top price for those…"

"Then you overpaid."

Through it all, the redhead had kept her cool, and now she calmly said to Tenew, "I told you they were too big to be fast enough."

The smile I gave her was genuine. "Spoken like a lady who knows her augmentations." I stood up and reached right over Tenew to offer her my hand. "I don't believe we've been introduced. I'm Jed Ecnirp."

She smiled up at me with enough wattage to melt a deep-frozen comet as she offered me her hand. Her touch sent a tingle up my arm and straight into my heart. "Melanada Tropess, but my friends call me Mela." She accented the second syllable of her name. Me-*LAN*-a-da.

"Mela. What a wonderfully melodious name."

Tenew, caught between us and most distinctly unhappy at being ignored, cleared his throat loudly.

I sat back down, not breaking eye contact with the beauty across from me. And just to irritate Tenew a little bit more, I said to her, "I would be honored if you would allow me to buy you dinner once I conclude my business here."

That was too much for the man who thought he ran things.

"You'll do no such thing," he exploded. Pointing to the two men still writhing on the floor, he told Mela, "See to their injuries already."

With that same calm confidence in which she'd spoken to Tenew a minute before, she said, "Medics are on the way." I hadn't seen her make a call, but the way she spoke convinced me she had been the one to summon them. Interesting. There was certainly more to her than met the eye. Neuroware with a commlink, at least.

Reluctantly turning my attention back to Tenew, I told him, "You know, in a way you are responsible for what happened to them, don't you think?"

"What... what are you talking about"

"It was on your order that they waylaid me last week, wasn't it?"

I could see him thinking about denying it. He wanted to, but after seeing how quickly I dropped his two thugs he was afraid of what I would do to him if and when I caught him. His thoughts played out on his face so clearly a blind man could have seen them. Finally, he swallowed and said, "Yeah, I did. That woman you was talking to is bad news. Don't no employee of mine need to have nothing to do with her."

And why was that, I wondered. Was she competing for the same business? Perhaps Tenew wasn't my only lead after all. And Nicollette was certainly more pleasant to deal with. But first...

"So you already consider me one of your men? Good. And now that I have returned from my jungle safari, I'm ready to go to work. I trust you haven't forgotten about our arrangement?"

You know, I was half hoping he would try to weasel out of our deal. I just really wanted an excuse to mess him up. I suspect he thought the same thing, too, which is why he looked relieved to be actually talking business finally.

"Of course I haven't. I'm a man of my word, Mr. Ecnirp. In fact, I have a warehouse full of dino armor that is just waiting to be shipped."

So that's how it was done. After my time with the Devil's

Rejects, I should have figured that much out. Herrig's World didn't have much of anything worth anything to the galaxy at large except minzite, but I could see where dino scales could at least be plausibly argued to be of interest to someone and thus worth exporting. A load of them would get me by the Trade Commission inspectors in orbit, anyway.

"Well now, that's mighty interesting. And whereabouts would the buyer be?"

He held up an index finger and wagged its side to side. "Ah, ah, ah. It doesn't work like that. I have certain procedures that I rigidly adhere to, and I make no exceptions for any man. You can agree to do things my way or we will not do business together. Is that clear?"

He was obviously relishing the feeling of being back in control, and I allowed him to hold on to that illusion while we watched a team of medics immobilize and load his two bio-augments onto floating structures and take them away.

When they were gone and the bar patrons had resumed their usual level of revelry, I burst his happy bubble by saying, "It's too late to go trying to impose conditions now. I've already demonstrated my good faith by going on your little sightseeing trip. If you try to back out now, I can't say as I'd be very happy."

He swallowed but managed not to look nervous. "All I'm saying is, in a business like this, I've found certain practices that make everything go smoother."

"What practices?"

I wasn't giving in an inch, and he knew it. "For one thing, until I have made use of a particular shipper's service a number of times, I require that an observer of my choice accompany him. Surely you can see how a man in my position needs to keep an eye on his assets."

I was liking this whole deal less and less, but since I'd already invested so much time in it, I figured I owed it to myself to try and see it through. "And who did you have in mind for this position?"

He actually looked like I'd caught him unprepared, like I'd asked a question he had no answer for. "Well, uh, normally it would be either Jifl or Marex, but you... uh... deprived me of their services for a time."

I let that one pass; I didn't want him getting sidetracked again just then.

"The other employee I've used in the past is on a run right now. I suppose you can wait until he gets back or one of the others is recovered."

I was about to tell him just how little I thought of that idea when Mela surprised us both by volunteering to go herself.

"I'll do it, Foral."

We both turned to look at her, although it's probably safe to say with different thoughts going through our heads.

"What? You told me yourself that the buyer is impatient," she said to him very reasonably. "And after what Jed -" She used my first name, in all the intimacy that it implied. "- did to Marex and Jifl, do you think anyone else is going to want to ride herd on him? Face it, you've got no one else who stands a chance of keeping him under control."

That statement bothered me for a couple of reasons. Why did she think I might need to be kept under control, and more importantly, how did she think she would do it? Her feminine wiles? I'm a ladies man, sure, but I'm my own man first.

Tenew's next argument, though, suggested that there was more in her arsenal than just sex, however.

"And who is going to look out for my wellbeing during your absence?"

Wellbeing? Perhaps I'd been wrong about why he had her with him. I was starting to suspect Mela was much more than she appeared.

"Look at all these gunslingers. Don't tell me you can't have a few of them watch your back until I return."

I could tell he didn't like the idea, but he seemed to settle on Mela going with me.

"Fine, have it your way. I assume you won't have a problem with her accompanying you, Mr. Ecnirp?"

I didn't. In fact, I found myself looking forward to finding out just what makes her tick. I didn't tell him that, though. What I said was, "Fair enough, I suppose, as long as I agree to the rest of your 'procedures'."

I had to remind him who was really in control, after all.

He was losing to both Mela and me, and it was leaving a bitter taste in his mouth that his expensive, foamy drink couldn't wash away. He downed it in a big gulp, anyway, before replying.

"There's nothing much more to it. Mela will give you your destination once you are underway, and she will handle recognition protocols with the buyers once you arrive. And, of course, you will not be allowed to make any detours along the way. I can't have my shippers being tempted to call any of their friends and make, um, alternate arrangements. You understand, I'm sure."

Oh, I understood, all right. He didn't want anyone stopping anywhere that had an ansible and placing an FTL call to any other buyers that might be interested in a shipload of tax-free minzite.

Of course, he had no way of knowing that I have my own ansible aboard the *Wah*. Expense is no barrier to keeping in touch with the Crown Prince, in the Emperor's eyes.

I told Tenew that those all sounded reasonable enough. Then, just like any other profit-hungry smuggler, I broached the all-important subject of payment. He offered a ridiculously low amount, I countered with twice that, and we met in the middle just as we'd both known we would.

"You will return here, and when Mela assures me that all went as planned, I'll pay you. I'm sure you can see understanding my position in this."

"Oh, I understand. I'm not crazy about it, though. I need to stock up on supplies, you know. How about half upfront?" Arguing, just like anyone worried about every credit would.

"No, I need to know you have a considerable incentive to return. And as for operating capital, that is one reason I sent you out with the clearing crew. Don't tell me you have already gambled all your pay away."

That pretty much ended our meeting. We made arrangements to have my ship loaded the following morning and I told him I should be ready for departure by late afternoon. When I asked Mela about dinner she thanked me for offering but said she owed it to Tenew to remain with him that evening. I got the impression she did it more out of the obligation of a paid bodyguard than any desire for his company, though. A very interesting woman, that Mela.

As for myself, I was still tired enough from my last day of clearing work that I decided to limit the rest of my evening to a few rounds of cards with some of my fellow Rejects and call it an early night. I didn't even try to find any female companionship for the night. I'd be shipping out with Mela soon enough.

CHAPTER 4

Most of the ceramic dino armor plates in my own hold were not, it turned out, the product of natural evolution. No, they were actually a thin shell of ceramic over refined minzite. Tenew had told me that the smuggler's hold in my ship wouldn't be needed, and he was right. I was carrying my illegal cargo nearly out in the open, thanks to some clever smuggler who had noticed that the natural ceramic and the highly valuable mineral had almost exactly the same density. Most remote scanning techniques couldn't tell the difference between real and false armor, so the game was on.

I learned this from the man who had come to oversee the loading of the shipment, an employee of Tenew's who never gave me his name. He was very talkative otherwise, though, and I learned quite a bit from him. Much more than he realized, I'm sure.

It turned out that there exists on Herrig's a small but thriving underground community of artisans who compete amongst themselves to create the most lifelike minzite replicas of the various types of dino armor, the larger the piece the better. This has been going on for generations on a small scale, but in the last couple of years demand for their products has reached literally astronomical proportions.

Another interesting tidbit I garnered from our conversation is that, of all the mining companies operating on Herrig's, Tar-Nevin Mining is practically the only one whose product was never exported in this manner.

Curiouser and curiouser, as the saying goes.

Could it be that Nicolette had walked away from me because she'd gotten wind that I was associated with known smugglers and she and her family were above such nefarious doings? It was something to think about.

A final piece of information I gleaned from the cargo-master was that he never saw any individual shipper return for another load in less than 6 weeks. This was especially interesting to me since I'd been unable to get any idea of what kind of round trip time I was looking at from either Tenew or Mela. He had been adamant about not revealing any details of my flight to me while I was in a position to tell anyone anything, and she had been playing the loyal employee and echoing the company Line.

What this three-week one-way flight time told me was that my destination was almost certainly well beyond the borders of the Empire of the Ninety-Nine Stars.

Someone outside the Empire was buying large quantities of minzite and had been doing so for a couple of years now; much larger quantities than anyone on Alphum suspected. That begged the question: why?

It's possible that whoever was buying it was using it to produce their very own line of anti-gravity or localized-gravity products and just wants to avoid paying the heavy export tax on the ore. There could be nothing more going on here than simple economic pressures can account for.

Maybe. Or may not be, as my Royal father likes to say.

Large quantities of minzite are also needed to build gravity weapons.

Gravity weapons, like the one that was used to destroy the planet Loralai back during the Spartan Insurrection, that killed over 2 billion people.

This case was potentially becoming about much more than lost revenue. While I could hope that it was nothing more than a relatively harmless tax dodge, I could not afford to take the chance that it wasn't.

Mela might be in for a much longer journey than she expected, because if what I suspected might happen did, I was going to make every effort to follow our mysterious buyer back to his base.

△△△

When Mela showed up at the *Wah*, she brought with her not a travel bag or three, but a half-dozen trunks, a couple of them very large.

I eyed her gear reproachfully. "Wow. I guess *that's* the difference between boys and girls. I always wondered what my mommy meant."

She laughed and it lit up her whole face. "If you think the way we travel is the only difference, we're both in for a very boring flight."

"You mean there's *more*? Really? Will you show me?" I gave her my patented, eager puppy dog eyes. She had trouble keeping a straight face in front of the porters that were loading her luggage. "Maybe, if you're a good boy."

"Oh, I'm good. I'm always good."

That was too much for her. She lost it then and her laughter rang throughout the ship like the sweetest music.

When she had recovered, I asked her, "Seriously, what's with all the trunks? Just how far away is our... um... rendezvous?"

"Oh, don't look so worried. I'm just a girl who likes her little touches of home, that's all. And besides, those two biggest cases contain real, honest-to-goodness, non-synthesized food."

"Really? Wow. I must be traveling with royalty. Way out here, that much real food's got to be worth a fortune."

She laughed again. "I like to indulge my appetites from time to time. And no offense to your ship, but I've never been a big fan of synthetic food."

I wanted to tell her to just wait until dinner but I held my tongue. Like so much else aboard my highly - and expensively - customized ship, my food synthesizer is top of the line. Only extremely sensitive and discriminating palates can tell its products from the real thing. It so far outclasses the grub machines that I'd been eating out of elsewhere as to not even be in the same class. I like my little luxuries, too, especially when I end up spending so much time in space.

"Well, if you can afford it."

"I can. Mr. Tenew may be a lot of things, but cheap isn't one of them."

I could have argued that, based on what he had agreed to pay me for my services, but I let it pass since the cargomaster was approaching.

He flipped me a lazy salute and said, "She's all yours, mate. Fifty-three containers, loaded and secured, with all the transit forms filed and cleared."

And that was that. Within another 20 minutes, the *Wah* was rising on her own minzite-coil-generated antigravity, and by the time we reached orbit our feet were being held to the deck by more minzite in the ship's localized-gravity generators. As I said, the stuff is invaluable to space-faring.

△△△

In keeping with its outward appearance, the interior of my ship is a study in serviceable-but-well-used. Nothing attracts the eye by its newness, yet nowhere are there signs of imminent catastrophe either. The deck plating is worn more in the middle of the corridors than along the edges and the furnishings are all of different ages.

In truth it *is* an older vessel, lovingly cared for by its previous owners yet never the recipient of expensive, unnecessary gadgetry.

That is, until I purchased it. Now it has the same look, but beneath that carefully preserved layer lies the work of some of the

Empire's foremost shipfitters. In engines, computers, defenses, armaments and other vital systems it is fit for royalty. I may enjoy flitting about the 99 Stars in the guise of an ordinary independent tramp freighter, but I always have several figurative aces up my sleeve.

Occasionally a real one, too, but that's a different story.

Of all the modifications I'd had done to the ship, though, perhaps the most important one was the one that hid in plain sight in the form of JD, the *Wah's* utility android. While limited-function labor droids are so commonplace that no one ever pays any attention to them, self-aware humanoid models are so rare that their presence always attracts attention. They are not only so expensive as to be beyond the means of a supposed hard-luck goodshauler like I posed as, anyone who did travel alone with one was automatically suspected of using it for perverse indulgences.

To set the record straight, I don't and never have.

What I have been known to have him assist me with is in the completion of quite a number of otherwise difficult or impossible missions, for there is much more to JD than his appearance suggests. To look at him you would see only his legally-mandated AI-identifying blue skin tone on an otherwise average body, but inside he was anything but ordinary. Not only did he run on one of the most advanced neural processors ever created, this processor was fully contained within him. This meant he could operate far from the ship without relying on a data connection to its computers. And not only could he employ this superb processing capacity to force his way into otherwise-inaccessible data vaults, he had the stealth capability to get himself to where he could make such access.

In addition to his plain usefulness, he was also one of my best friends and most trusted allies. He and I have been through a lot together.

Although I usually travel with only JD for company, the *Wah* can comfortably house 6 people. In addition to several common areas of various function, she boasts sleeping accommodations in the form of two double cabins and two larger, more inviting ones.

It was to the other single that I had JD deliver Mela's luggage, being the gentleman that I am and not presuming to install her in my own room *a priori*.

Mela had merely nodded her head at this arrangement, knowing as well as I that it was subject to revision at any time.

After having shown her through the living spaces, we were both on the bridge. Although the *Wah* is, like nearly every other starship, almost completely automated, it still retains provisions for the hands-on control of all of its major functions. This is nowhere more evident than here, where four different stations are arranged in a semi-circle around the central shipmaster's seat and console.

As I took my customary position there and I gestured toward the navigator's domain on my left. "That would be the most logical place for you, o knower of our unknown trajectory."

She looked over the array of screens and controls with a bewildered expression of someone being asked to perform a task which they are not only unschooled in but wish they had not even known existed until that very moment. "I... uh... don't actually know anything about flying a starship."

Yeah, I'd noticed. "But you do at least have some coordinates for me, don't you?"

She pulled a tiny data card out of a pocket and held it up. "Mr. Tenew gave me this, but he said not to give it to you until we had left this system. We're supposed to pretend to head towards the central worlds, then change course once we're in hyperspace."

"Fair enough, I suppose." I punched in our destination as Borma IV, pretty much at random. "There. As soon as those ITC guys decide whether to harass us or not we'll be out of here."

"Oh, they won't. Trust me, Mr. Tenew pays more than enough to make sure of that."

So, another interesting data point to add to my collection, but not one which surprised me. I'd known that the corruption was spread all amongst everyone who had anything to do with the minzite trade. When the time comes to take down this whole system, a lot of heads are going to roll. And Mela was right, of course.

Our clearance came through almost immediately. The inspectors must be awfully bored, because I doubt they've done their real job in a long time.

I kept us in hyperspace for 20 minutes before dropping out into the empty void far from any stars, which was more than long enough to put us far beyond the range of any tracking sensors based around Herrig's World. With a gesture towards a specific section of the navigation console, I then told Mela, "Alright, it's your turn. Flip up that access cover over there and insert your data card."

Once she did so, I could see on one of my screens that the card contained nothing but one set of coordinates. My nav comp knew only that there was a red dwarf star there - the most common thing in the galaxy, even out here on the rim. If there were any planets, habitable or not, was unknown. Just on the off-chance that the card had been used for the same purpose before, though, I silently asked JD to run a forensic data recovery program to see if there was any erased information on it that might be retrievable. It turned out there wasn't, but it never hurts to try.

I acted surprised when I said, "Oh, wow, this will take us a long way past the border. And at best speed it'll take us about two and a half weeks to get there. But I guess you knew that, considering how much luggage you brought." I smiled to take any sting out of my comment.

It must have worked, too, because she responded with a grin of her own. "Actually, Foral told me it would take at least three weeks. This ship must be a little faster than it looks."

No, actually it's a *lot* faster than it looks. I could have made the run in about 13 days if I pushed it, but I didn't want to tell her that. "Yeah, the previous owner was some kind of hotshot mechanic. He really tweaked-out the hyperdrive."

She put on a fake pout. "That's too bad."

"Oh, and why is that?"

Her response was a raised eyebrow and coy grin.

△△△

The next two and a half weeks passed all too quickly. Mela and I quickly discovered that we thoroughly enjoyed each other's company, but I suspect I only learned as much about the real her as she did of me. I'm not the only person in this galaxy who was less than forthcoming about my past and who the real me is, I suppose.

The most unsettling part about that is that I really needed to know just what she meant when she told Tenew that she could keep me under control. When I questioned her about it in an off-hand way all she would say is that I better hope I never found out. Surreptitious scans had revealed not a single implant in her, but yet I could not help but recall how I'd been convinced it was her who called for the medics after I just dropped Tenew's augmented bodyguards.

All this could add up to only one thing, I was afraid. I hoped I was wrong.

△△△

After nearly three weeks of anticipation I'd come up with quite a few possibilities as to how the upcoming encounter might take place. In what was probably the best imaginable scenario I would be led directly to a planet where I would discover a thriving manufacturing center for all things minzite-related and a single ansible call to the ICT would set all things right. Not highly likely, but it was a pleasant thought.

On the other side of the spectrum was my fear that we would emerge far outside the Empire smack dab in the middle of a vast armada that was in the process of arming itself with a host of gravity weapons. This seemed to be at least possible, based on what I'd pieced together since arriving on Herrig's World. The problem was, there was likely nothing I could do about it short of sending in colossal numbers of navy ships and starting an inter-galactic war.

The one thing I had not imagined happening was, of course, what did.

The coordinates brought us out of hyperspace well above the ecliptic plane of a rock and gravel system. This made it easy to scan for planets, of which there was only one. Other than this very close-in gas giant, there was only a broad disc of asteroids that spanned from 1 astronomical unit out to 6 AU.

That was a *lot* of rock. If there was a habitat hidden somewhere in amongst all that, and if it was even halfway trying to shield its emissions, it would take a full naval recon group to find it any-time this side of eternity.

For that matter, there could be a dozen battle fleets in there and I'd never know it. Someone could be *building* a fleet there, too. There was certainly enough raw material floating around.

"Oh, wow. I've heard about this place but I had no idea it was so big."

Mela's awe was understandable. I had a view of the system up on the big screen, and it sure was a sight to behold. Her words con-firmed something else I'd suspected, too. This was her first deliv-ery run.

"Well, I got us here. Now what?"

"Now we broadcast the recognition code on a specific channel and wait for someone to meet us."

These she had memorized, and in no time we were transmit-ting a loop of the code phrase. I had all sensors on high alert and sat back to wait.

"Any idea what happens next?" I asked casually, like I didn't really care what the exact procedure was, but in reality I was any-thing but unconcerned. This star system had 'secret base' written all over it, and I was convinced by now that there was nothing so innocent as cheating the Empire out of some tax money going on.

"He said it shouldn't take too long. A ship will dock with us and take our cargo. That's it. Then we head back. Oh, he did tell me to tell you that we are to leave as soon as the transfer is done. One of his shippers tried to wait around, probably wanting to see where the other ship was going. They blew him up."

Of course they did.

For as long as humanity has been in space - over 1,600 years - there have been persistent rumors of a race of man-like space faring aliens called Rolumands, or something like that. They are supposedly a very shy, reclusive species, and the reason no one has ever made official contact with them, so the stories go, is because their ships all make use of a perfect cloaking device. Invisible to all sensors, they travel the galaxy at will, going about their alien business in their alien way, with no one knowing they are there.

I would *kill* to have a cloaking device like that.

My ship has certain stealth capabilities, but any vessel in powered flight gives off emissions that can be detected by sufficiently determined sensors. And even when coasting, a fusion-powered craft - like the *Wah* - emits neutrinos from its reactor. No known technology can entirely mask this.

So there was not going to be any pressing of a magic button followed by me stealthily shadowing the ore back to its hidden base. I had to come up with another way of finding out where the minzite was going, and I had to do it right away.

I was assuming that the vessel my cargo was transferred to would remain in the star system. With hundreds of planets worth of rock to hide amongst, the system was perfect for any kind of clandestine activity.

But if I couldn't follow it back home, I'd never know to what nefarious purpose so much ore was being put to.

The computer's announcement that a large freighter and an even larger pair of warships of unknown design were approaching us at high speed snapped me out of my reverie. I was down to ten minutes to come up with a way of tracking them.

Then it hit me. The Rolumand's stealth capabilities are rivaled only by Sams. All I had to do was convince him to help.

Now, you have to understand something about Sam. His sole purpose of existence, as far as anyone has ever gotten him to admit, is preserving the Tarkle royal line. He is the ultimate bodyguard: immensely powerful, possessed of fantastic capabilities, loyal, ever alert and always present. All this is great, wonderful, and has saved my life on innumerable occasions.

It's that last part, though, the one about him never leaving me, that I've often wished he was the least bit flexible about. His presence has never bothered me; he's been there my whole life. I'm not embarrassed to do anything with him around, not even when I have a woman or two for company. But there have been times when his covert recon capability could have helped me, and I'm not talking about scoping the cards in another player's hand.

He's adamant, though. According to him, almost every Tarkle has asked him at some point to leave him alone long enough to go gather some much-needed intel, and he's never done so. He will always remain with his protectee, period.

(Sam, I really need your help here.)

((In what way, Sire?))

(I need you to follow the ore freighter that's about to rendezvous with us back to its base when it leaves.)

Sam's mental tone is always rather flat, but I swear I almost heard a note of humor in his reply. ((You know I cannot do that, yet you keep trying. It must be a family trait.))

(Look, this isn't like all those other times. If I'm right, these guys could be building a fleet armed with gravity weapons, planet-busters that could conceivably destroy even Alphum.))

((But you do not know that for certain.))

(No, I don't. That's why I need you to find out where their base is, so I can sneak in there and learn what they're doing with all this minzite.)

((You ask me to do this even when you know what my response must be.))

(Listen, you told me you exist to preserve the Empire.)

((Actually, I've told you that my purpose is to preserve the

Tarkle bloodline.))

(Okay, sure. Isn't that the same thing? And what would happen to the Empire if Alphum were destroyed?)

((The bloodline would survive. I will always ensure that.))

I wished I had time to dig deeper into that comment, but I knew better. Countless other Tarkles have tried and failed to get him to explain the why of that.

(Come on, I'll hide in hyperspace and be perfectly safe.)

((I cannot leave you, Prince Edj. What you ask is not possible.))

He can be so frustrating sometimes, especially when he says things like that and you just know you'll never get any kind of explanation out of him. My father warned me that there would be times when I'd wish I could knock some sense into Sam.

My father, whom Sam is with even while he's with me, too. The figurative light bulb came on over my head with that thought.

(Alright, fine. So tell me again how it is that you cannot leave me and at the same time cannot leave Father either.)

((I exist in all times, from your perspective, and therefore can project myself into any time. If I happen to already be manifest in a particular time when I need to be elsewhere, I . . . Very good, Sire. Well done.))

I was glad I was sitting down just then, let me tell you. Praise from Sam is just about as rare as solid sunlight.

(So you'll do it?)

((Since, as you say, there is a high probability of a threat to the stability of the Empire, in this one isolated instance I will place myself at your disposal.))

(You're the greatest, pal.)

I couldn't help but let out a heartfelt sigh of relief. It was only after that that I remembered Mela, who was staring at me with an utterly inscrutable look on her beautiful face. To cover my lapse I said, "I can't wait to get this part over with."

Her expression didn't change, and I just had time to begin to wonder what was wrong with her when she gave me the greatest shock of my life.

She asked, "Who's Sam?"

CHAPTER 5

All of a sudden, all my suspicions about Mela were confirmed, plus at least one I hadn't even considered. Her confidence that she could keep me under control, her employment as Tenew's bodyguard - it all made sense. She was a psionic, just as I'd feared. There's nothing in this galaxy more dangerous than a person who can slip into your head and do unthinkable things to your mind. And there's no defense against it either, which makes it even worse.

If that was all there was to her it would be bad enough. But no, she just had to go and be so strongly telepathic that she could eavesdrop on mine and Sam's conversation.

For the very first time in my life I was truly frightened. I've faced some of the biggest, baddest, toughest, ugliest, fastest and most skilled fighters this galaxy has ever come up with and never known the slightest fraction of the terror that this beautiful woman, whom I've been sharing my ship - my cabin - with for two and a half weeks, instilled in me with two simple words.

I briefly considered trying to lie to her, telling her that Sam was just a nickname I sometimes used for JD and that I was communicating with him via implant, but rejected the idea right away. She'd heard our entire conversation; Sam and I had both given too much away. All I could do was play the hand I'd been dealt, and every card I was holding had the word 'truth' writ bold across it.

But truth comes in many flavors. I chose the one that would hopefully impress upon her the futility of attacking my mind.

"Sam is a sentient black hole who is obsessed with keeping me alive and his existence a secret. Now that you know about him, you have two choices: submit to the Imperial Secrets Protection Policy or refuse to. Do you know what the ISPP is?"

"No."

"Hmm, and here I thought you might since it involves a high-level psionic implanting a psych block that prevents you from disclosing any aspect of his existence. The problem is, I don't think that can be done to another psionic without causing great pain and risking permanent brain damage."

Her flat expression gave nothing away. "And if I refuse?"

My voice went cold, too. "Sam absorbs you, and even the quarks that make up your body cease to exist in this universe."

Before she could answer, JD informed us that the freighter was on final docking approach. I gave him permission to proceed, then told Mela, "You've got until the transfer is done to decide."

I made myself turn and leave the bridge without looking at her, afraid of what I might see, afraid of what I might do.

***

The cargo transfer was handled quickly and professionally, and it was completed in short order. When I returned to the bridge Mela appeared not to have moved at all. She didn't look at me when I took my seat and took us into hyperspace.

After another minute of silence I gave up on waiting for her to say anything. "You know, I probably never would have caught on if you hadn't said anything," I said quietly, staring at my console.

"I wish I hadn't."

I finally looked at her. Her eyes were hard and there was the look of a powerful beast preparing to fight an even more powerful adversary in her posture.

"What are you going to do with me, Your Highness?"

"First off, there'll be none of that formal court talk. We are way out here, two people who've been living as lovers for weeks. I'm still Edj."

"You're not the Edj I thought I knew."

"And you are not the Mela I thought I knew, either. We both

had our reasons for hiding who we really are, but now that everything's out in the open all we can do is move forward. Now, I have a job to do and you can either help me or I can put you in stasis until I turn you over to the psi-corp. And keep this in mind: Sam is completely without sentiment when it comes to protecting me. Try anything with my head and it'll be the last thing you ever do."

I didn't like threatening her, but what could I do? She had to be made aware of exactly what her situation was.

Thankfully, she saw it for that, too, and didn't hold it against me. "Look, I have no intention of hurting you or revealing who you are."

I was glad to hear her say that. I just hoped I could believe her.

Once more talking to each other as friends, I told her what I had learned on Herrig's and my suspicions. When she told me that my estimates of how much ore was being smuggled were actually too low, it made me that much more convinced that something Not Nice was going on.

"But who would want to build such terrible weapons? Why? And where is all the money coming from?"

All her questions were good ones, ones that I wanted answers to myself. "I don't know yet, but I fully intend to find out."

One good thing about Mela knowing who I am is that I didn't have to hide all my resources and capabilities from her anymore. This made it much easier for me to place an FTL call to my father to let him know what I learned, suspected, and intended to do. The one part I left out was any mention of Mela being psionic. I just couldn't bear to put what I knew about her out there like that.

I thought, back then, that there would be plenty of time for that later, if I hadn't come up with a third option by the time we were done.

$$\triangle\triangle\triangle$$

"I still can't believe it," she said when I was done with my call.

"What's that?"

"That I just watched the man I woke up beside this morning place a call straight through to the Emperor!" She tried to hide it, but I still caught a hint of unexpected admiration in her voice.

"Yeah, well, R.H.I.P."

"What?" Her tone changed to confusion.

"Rank Hath Its Privileges." I gave her a grin and a wink before adding, "But what they don't tell you is that it comes with a lot more gilded chains than door keys."

"So is that why you fly around the Empire in this old tub, to avoid all the pressures of life on Alphum?"

I looked around the bridge when she said that, an exaggerated look of damaged pride showing in my wide eyes and voice. "An old tub? The *Wah?* Bite your tongue, wench." I couldn't keep it up, though, and broke out in a heartfelt laugh.

We both needed the release after our earlier tensions. It felt good.

ΔΔΔ

While we were waiting for Sam's return Mela talked JD and I into joining her in a game of triple-ping-pong in the *Wah's* small lounge. This was one of her favorite games, she said, but finding quality opponents was always a challenge. I told her she might still be looking after she saw me play, which brought a mischievous grin to her face.

"That would be okay, too. The game's better when one person can control the play."

I shot her a grin of my own back as I said, "Alright, but don't get too upset when it turns out you're not the one in control."

She spun her racquet in the palm of her hand and looked at JD as she asked me, "Is there something else I should know about him?"

I laughed. "Oh, lots, but most of it is classified. I can tell you this, though: if he doesn't dial down his reaction speed to merely augmented human rates, there is absolutely no chance either of us will beat him."

She turned to really look at JD. "Are you really that advanced?"

"You have no idea, Miss Tropess."

To me she said, "I'll bet having him around has come in handy a few times."

I laughed again. "A few. Like, for instance," I said as I made the first serve, "the time one of his unexpected abilities saved the life of Dornathion's Prime Apostle's son."

Mela easily returned my somewhat inexpert lob and deftly sent it JD's way. "Dornathion? Isn't that the world that follows that really strict religion that doesn't allow its people to receive any medical care?"

"Well, they all want to get to their Heaven as soon as... Vac-sucker! I almost had that one." I bent over to pick up the ball that Mela had sent just a few inches beyond my reach. "Your point. Anyway, yeah, I was visiting in my... Not again! I see your ploy now, trickster. You want me to divide my attention. You tell her, JD. I need to concentrate on my game."

"Certainly, Sire." JD had no problem talking while expertly countering every return Mela made and even scoring the occasional point against her. "As Prince Edj was saying, he was on a State visit and had been invited to accompany Madam Orophresa's son on a sailboat tour around the planet's famous Prophet's Cove. When His Highness made mention of my ability to operate such a vessel, Jaspoir insisted I come along as well."

My neuroware's download of triple-ping-pong skills had finished and was running by this point and I was able to execute a double-bounce flawlessly, much to Mela's surprise. "Didn't see that one coming, did you? See, I'm a quick learner."

"Or something," she said with a suspicious grin and a laugh. To distract her, I told JD to finish his story.

"It was very fortunate for him that he had, for in the course of our excursion the young man insisted on going for a swim despite his knowledge that the water was inhabited by a dangerous variety of predatory fish that uses electricity to stun its prey."

"Let me guess," Mela said, putting a twist on the ball that sent it under JD's guard, scoring her a point against him. "He got stung."

"Well played, Miss Tropess. Yes, he did. His heart went into cardiac arrhythmia. And despite Prince Edj's insistence to the contrary, Jaspoir's survival can be attributed as much to his own action as to my own."

"Modesty from Edj? You've got to be joking."

"Not at all, ma'am. As you may be aware, constructs such as myself are much denser that humans. I cannot swim in liquid water; thus I was still aboard the boat when the incident occurred. Had Prince Edj not risked his own safety by immediately swimming to Jaspoir and towing him to the boat I would not have been able to pull him onboard and administer the appropriate electrostimulation to restore proper cardiac function."

"So you can shock someone back to life? Impressive. I guess you are full of hidden talents."

"I was built with a wide range of capabilities not customarily included in standard androids."

"Yeah," I said, sending him a setup that he used to score the winning point against Mela. "Including being able to beat you at your own game."

"I see that. Although I wonder just what else might have contributed..."

I grinned at her. "Surely you don't think I cheated, do you?"

She laughed. "I'm just saying I think there's more to both of you than meets the eye."

"A very astute observation, Miss Tropess. Care for a rematch?"

We played again, and JD beat us both handily.

△△△

It was close to an hour after we left the freighter and its warship escorts before Sam informed us that the minzite had been delivered to a base hidden inside an asteroid the size of a dwarf planet, some 800 miles in diameter in his estimation.

"Oh, man, they could be building anything in there," was Mela's assessment of that news.

For his part, Sam seemed to have accepted my acceptance of her knowledge of him, for he spoke to both of us without any mention of any consequences to her knowing. It made me wonder if he knew something he wasn't saying. I would have asked him, but I knew he'd deny it. He's like that when it comes to talking about the future.

Anyway, with his help I was soon able to locate the planetoid in the sensor records the *Wah* had made of the system before we left. It was surrounded by thousands of smaller rocks, all moving in chaotic patterns. The only reason all of it hadn't long since coagulated into larger bodies had to be the destabilizing influence of the primary star's not-too-distant binary companion.

(Were there any signs of other ships?) I asked, wanting as complete a strategic picture as possible.

((Yes. In addition to the two combat vessels that accompanied the freighter, which took up positions in defense of the planetoid, there were also another pair of large civilian vessels on its surface.))

Mela got a faraway look on her face for a moment, then said, "Sorry, I forgot for a minute that while Sam can hear my telepathy, you can't. I was asking him if he saw anything that looked like a factory. You know, if they are just making cheap gravity plates or something. That's what all of us back on Herrig's thought it was all about."

((I followed the freighter as far as a large opening in the planetoid's crust, as was the prince's instruction. I could feel by its gravitational displacement that it is merely a relatively thin shell surrounding a metallic construct of some sort, but I did not investigate further.))

Mela and I just looked at each other, the same thought clearly in her head as was my own. Like I said before, there are times when I wish I could knock some sense into Sam. It's not his fault, really, though. I, and as far as I can tell most all my ancestors, tended to think that since Sam talks like us, he must think like us as well. The thing is, he is about as alien a mind as there could ever be. He's not human, and any similarities in our thought processes are merely an artifice he employs so that we can understand him. One of the side effects of this is that he tends to take a very literal interpretation of anything that is said to him. Another is that he does not read anything more into a statement than is explicitly said.

Needless to say, he can be very frustrating to deal with sometimes. It gets to me sometimes, and I've known him all my life and grew up on my father's stories of their adventures together.

To Mela, having had no preparation for his peculiarities, it was maddening.

"But why didn't you look inside? You were right there. You could have told us everything we need to know."

((I did what was asked of me. You now know where this base is and that it is not being used for the construction of a fleet armed with planet-busters.))

"Okay, yeah, but we don't know what they are doing there. Can you go back and get a better look around inside? Please?"

I could have told her not to waste her time, but I figured she might as well learn for herself how fruitless it is trying to talk him into doing recon. My one victory aside, I've never had any success.

She didn't either. It took her a good fifteen minutes of arguing before she finally admitted defeat. I managed to put that same time to good use, at least, since I *knew* the only way we were going to find out what was being built inside a giant hollow rock hidden way out in the unclaimed space beyond the Empire was for me to go in there and see for myself.

Now that I knew where it was and that there were only two warships guarding it, I was able to plot a course to it that would, with any luck, get the *Wah* close enough for me to jump from one to the other.

"He's impossible! Why do you even put up with him anyway?"

Ah, so she finally gave up. "Um, well, let's see. For starters, there's the fact that he's the best bodyguard in the universe…"

"Yeah, I can respect that," she said, nodding her head in agreement.

"So anyway," I said, getting us back on course, "I've come up with a way to get a look inside that there eggshell."

She looked at me like she wasn't convinced. "Oh really? Do tell."

"Well, even without one of those famous Rolumand cloaking shields, the *Wah* can run pretty dark, especially with her reactor shut down. I've drawn up a course to get us within a few thousand miles of the base, where we'll 'land' on one of the bigger rocks. What?" She was looking at me with one eyebrow cocked up and her head slightly tilted. I could tell she already thought there was something funny about my plan.

"I don't know much about flying a spaceship, especially in a dense asteroid field like this, but don't you need engine power to zig and zag? There's no way even your souped-up royal yacht can fly through this much stuff without taking a few hits and you want to do it without shields, too?"

She didn't accuse me of being crazy, but I could hear it in her voice.

"Okay, you're right that the engine and shields are powered by the fusion plant. But that baby gives off neutrinos that can be detected, so I can't get us anywhere close with it running. Fortunately for us, we have another way to maneuver the ship and protect it from collisions. I believe you've met him. His name is Sam."

So then I had to explain that my multi-talented companion is such a master of mass and gravity manipulation that he can precisely emit a gravity beam so narrowly focused that it can pull a starship around but not be detected from anywhere but directly astern. Between that and his ability to absorb mass directly into himself without it going into orbit around him in an accretion disk, and thus giving off any Hawking radiation, he can both maneuver and protect us without setting off anyone's sensors.

"If you say so," was her response to all that. "So then what? After we park and hide, I mean?"

I steeled myself for what I knew was coming next by taking a deep breath. "Then I suit up and have Sam fly me and JD over to the base where-"

"Not by yourselves you don't!"

I'd prepared myself for her to disagree with me, but the vehemence of her objection still rattled my ears and shook my wisdom teeth.

"Yes, by ourselves. We don't know what-"

"Not going to happen. There's no way you're leaving me-"

Two can play the interruption game. "It's too dangerous. I need you safe aboard to the *Wah* to relay my findings."

"Nice try, but I'm going. I can take care of myself."

"Sam will make sure I don't die. You don't have any such-"

"No one but you does and we risk our lives every day! This is important to the Empire, Prince Edj. You can't stop me from doing my part."

It was gratifying to see that she shared my concerns about the gravity of the situation, even if she couldn't have picked a worse time to remind me of it. "I can and will stop you. There's no need for you to risk-"

"Are you capable of torturing someone?"

That question was such a non sequitur that I just froze up, not knowing where she was coming from or heading to with it.

"Are you?"

"I... I suppose... No, I don't think so. Now, what kind of question is that, anyway? What does it have to do with you not coming with me?"

"We're here for vital information. Are you just going to go over there and nicely ask the first person you come across what they're building in the secret base? Think that'll work, do you?"

I shook my head. "No, of course not. I'm going after computer files and everything else our scanners can record."

"Without being seen or setting off any alarms?"

"It's not a perfect solution, but I've got to-"

"Look at me."

She said that with such a tone of compulsion in her voice that I immediately looked up from my console and over toward her. At least, where I thought she'd just been sitting. I glanced all around the bridge, not seeing her anywhere. "Where did you go?"

I blinked, and she was sitting right where I thought she had been. "Nowhere. I was right here all along. And now I know you're thinking how much psionics creep you out."

I was speechless. I had been thinking just that. It didn't take her much more arguing to convince me to let her come with me.

ΔΔΔ

To avoid any chance of being detected I brought us out of hyperspace on the opposite side of the sun from the secret facility. The transition to or from that pseudo-dimension lets loose a lot of stray radiation, but unless they had sensor drones deployed around the system, the stellar dodge would cover for that.

I then used the inertia-canceling normal space drive to accelerate us to half of light speed before shutting down the fusion reactor. The storage battery, which was fully charged, was then the only source of power for all internal ship's functions. Any maneuvering we would need to do from this point on, and decelerating when we got close to the target, were all on Sam now.

During the run-up to speed and hour-long ballistic coast across the system I familiarized Mela with the features and operation of the top-end vacuum armor suits we were going to wear.

These were not the space suits from the locker just inside the air-lock, the cheap, older model ones kept there in accordance with the theme of the ship's disguise.

No, these were the two I kept hidden away in one of the many smuggler's holds. Once again I was relieved not to have to hide anything from her, for these were the same practically-invisible suits worn by the elite Imperial Commandos. Each one costs as much as a small spacecraft, and indeed, that is exactly what they are. Relatively lightweight but feature-packed, protected by active defenses as well as their own shield generator in addition to micro-thin, diamond-hard armor plates, and sheathed in metamaterials that render them nearly invisible across a broad swath of the EM spectrum, these are what the best dressed soldiers in the entire Empire wear on their most dangerous missions.

Being the prince does have some advantages.

Mela caught on quick as I explained the few controls to her. The suit is designed to be as intuitive to use as possible, and its built-in AI can handle nearly every function on its own - the idea being that a soldier wearing it is going to have more important things on his mind than basic functions like when to activate the grippers in his boot soles or filtering eye-searing blasts through the faceplate.

Even so, I thought she was going to change her mind about accompanying us after only a minute or two sealed inside it.

"It's the closeness of everything. I can't think of anything but running out of air! I see the icons and stuff at the edge of the faceplate and it makes me feel like the whole universe has shrunk to the size of the suit. Full disclosure: I'm claustrophobic. I can't stand being cooped up in a suit. The sooner I can get out of here, the better. If we weren't trying to save the Empire, I'd sooner let you stab me in the eye than make me wear this thing."

Who would have known she was claustrophobic?

Her determination to serve the Empire is what eventually got her through her anxiety. I told her that I could handle it, but that argument fell on deaf ears. "You know what I mean. You need my talents for this mission, and I'm not going to let you down."

By the time Sam exercised his almost magical control over mass, inertia, and gravity to bring the ship to a halt relative to the surface of my chosen asteroid, she was insistent that she'd conquered her fears and was as ready as she'd ever be.

"Once we step out the airlock there's no turning back," I warned her. I think maybe I had some faint foreboding about what was about to happen to her even then. I wish it had been strong enough to make me stop her.

"I know. Let's do this..."

△△△

Our crossing of the asteroid field between the *Wah* and the secret base began uneventfully enough. With Sam invisible but undeniably present between and ahead of us, Mela, JD and I were irresistibly pulled along by the tiny fraction of his mass that he allowed to bleed through into our universe. He swiftly accelerated us to a cruising velocity that would cover the few thousand miles in a matter of a half hour or so.

Once we were coasting he was free to resume his primary task of protecting me. In this case, that meant deflecting or absorbing any rock or piece of gravel in my path. For the most part, this also protected Mela and JD, but I was and am always his highest priority.

We were no more than a hundred miles from the hollow planetoid when we encountered an especially dense patch of debris. There were so many individual pieces and neither our armor's active defense micro-blasters, shields, or Sam's best intentions could protect all of us.

A single grain of sand made it through all of our defenses and impacted Mela's suit. At the speed we were traveling, it packed more kinetic energy than any bullet ever fired from a rifle.

CHAPTER 6

F ree-flying in space always reminds me of my first experience in open vacuum when I was a boy of twelve. At some
point during every excursion since then my mind has always drifted back to the occasion of my much-anticipated first
space-walk.

As a scheduled part of my education, I'd been looking forward
to this event for years, it seems like. Yet the closer that date
drew, I found myself growing more and more nervous, not that I
would ever admit that to anyone. Oh no, not brave Young Prince
Edj, heir to the Crystal Throne of the Empire of the Ninety-Nine
Stars. I had an image to maintain and showing the slightest hint of
unprincely hesitation in anything was just not to be allowed. My
head was ever held high, my hand steady and firm, no matter who
or what I faced.

But in the most secret, hidden recesses of my heart, I quailed
at the thought of stepping out of a perfectly good spaceship and
exposing my precious Royal self to the harsh, unforgivingly air-
less unpressurized vacuum of space, encased in only the meager
protection of a flimsy spacesuit. For the first time in my life I
would be deliberately putting myself at risk beyond the magical
abilities of Sam to protect me from.

What would happen, I wondered, lying awake late at night, if
my suit sprung a leak and all my air rushed out? What if a thruster
misfired and shot me into the path of a starship traveling at an
interplanetary velocity? What if, what if...

The mind of an intelligent, well-educated 12-year-old prince is a fertile place where fears, nurtured by the illogic of the half-asleep brain, can spring fully formed from the most innocuous of seeds. No amount of daytime knowledge can fully dispel these nocturnal ramblings once they have been sufficiently nourished and cultivated by successive nightly feedings, and they secretly haunted me all through the preparations for that monumental milestone event.

Something strange, something so completely unexpected that I had never even considered it a possibility, happened to me as I drifted out of that airlock, though.

I was calmly, serenely at peace. The voice of my instructor faded from my ear, the thundering of my constrained pulse slowed to a gentle flow, all my wild imaginings evaporated. I felt no more anxiety, and all of my previous worries suddenly seemed no more substantial than a faded, dusty hologram.

I was free from gravity, and so much more besides. The bright jewels of the stars were suddenly at my fingertips. The once immense distance between me and them contracted to the width of a thought. The universe was mine in a way I had never before imagined. I was the universe, and the universe was me.

That wondrous sense of connectedness has never completely left me, even after three decades. Many times in the intervening years I've stepped out into space for no other reason than to recreate that feeling.

Not even a hail of projectiles zooming at me at incredible velocities, with all the implied risk that entailed, could keep me from losing myself in the serenity of being in free space.

But a scream of shock and alarm from my companion did.

ΔΔΔ

Even in stealth mode our suits are able to stay in contact with each other via automatic directed-laser comms, as long as there is a reasonably uninterrupted line of sight between us. That's how I could see, at the edge of my faceplate, a displayed schematic of Mela's suit which showed that it had sustained a non-penetrating but high-energy kinetic impact to its right shin.

"God, my leg! My leg's hit! Oh, oh…"

"Mela, stay calm," I told her firmly. As my combat instructor taught me, often an injured comrade will respond to a firm but calm tone of command better than anything else. "Your suit's not leaking. You took a hit but your armor stopped it. You'll be okay." ((Sam, slow us down, a *lot!*))

"It feels like it's shattered and… and now my leg is going cold and numb. There *is* a leak!"

"Stop that's talk! You're going to be fine. There's no leak, that's just your suit giving you a pain block."

The telemetry relayed to me from her suit showed an icon indicating this, just as it would be showing in her own field of vision, but she probably couldn't interpret what she was seeing even if she was calm enough to pay it any attention.

What I had no way of knowing yet was just how bad her injury was. An impact hard enough to fracture the armor plate would certainly have transmitted some of its kinetic energy into the flesh beneath it. The question was, did it merely bruise her or did it shatter her lower leg bones into a million pieces, or anything in between?

Fortunately, we were still far enough away from the planetoid and its patrolling defenders for me to risk momentarily firing my maneuvering thrusters a couple of times without much chance of being detected. Mela was curled into a ball with both hands holding her injured right shin by the time I got to her. I grabbed hold of her right arm, which I could only see because of the augmented-reality overlay provided by my visor.

I didn't need any such help to see the damaged lower leg of her armor. When the impact shattered the protective plate it also disrupted the cloaking material which had, until then, channeled light and certain frequencies of radiation around the solid matter it encased. While not much good against reasonably competent electronic sensors, when undamaged it could fool the human eye into thinking there was nothing there.

That could be a problem once we got inside the installation, but there was nothing I could do about that.

The same was probably true of whatever injury lay underneath it, too, but I nonetheless had to know how bad it was. With my handheld multiscanner set to low power there was very little chance of it giving us away, which was one reason I'd wanted to close the distance between us.

"You are one lucky woman, my dear."

"I don't feel so lucky right now," she stammered. Her pain was palpable through her voice.

I held the scanner up so she could see it. "This says your leg is banged up but not broken. In my book, after taking a hit at this speed, that counts as lucky."

"If you say so."

"I do. You'll be fine. Your suit's pain-blocker field will take care of the hurt and you should still be able to walk even in normal gravity. Now come on, we've got some criminal's secret who-knows-what construction base to infiltrate. Are you with me?"

She was, of course. I wished I could have sent her back, but she wouldn't have gone even if I could have.

Sam brought us to a touchdown just over the planetoid's horizon from the two civilian spacecraft and the giant hole into its interior. We had all agreed that there was far too great a chance of being detected anywhere closer. The gravity there was much less than you would expect on a body that size; if I hadn't already known it was hollow, that would have clued me in.

The surface composition was of deep-frozen ices, explaining why it had been so easy for the bad guys to hollow it out. It also meant that it was going to be very hard to walk on. Without anything for the electromagnets in our boots to adhere to, and it being far too risky to use the minzite-based micro-focused grippers, every step was liable to send us bouncing off into space.

"Be very careful how you move," I warned Mela. "We don't need you going into orbit.

"Okay," I said next, taking stock of the situation to distract her - and myself - from the unforeseen difficulty. "Here's what we'll do. First I'm going to send JD over with the multi-scanner to get a good look around, both outside and in. We'll sit here, really still-like, until he gets back, and then we'll make for the most likely target."

"Sounds like a plan." I could hear her sigh. "Standing still like this, in the middle of nowhere on some gods-forsaken ice planet isn't helping my claustrophobia. Just a heads up."

"Look at me." I carefully turned to face her and took her hands in mine. "You're doing fine. You'll make it through this, I promise. Right now you just need something to focus your mind on. Why don't you tell me something about the real Melanada? What was it like growing up with your, um, talents?"

JD activated his full stealth mode and disappeared, and she did just that.

"I was born on Svartholm," she began, "the only child of a hard-working middle-class couple. My mother had me when she was almost 60, after being told all her life she was infertile and would never have children. My birth was hailed by the community as a miracle; they said my mam was touched by Freya and Frey, the nature gods they all pray to there.

"Well, their 'miracle girl' talk turned into accusations that maybe I was a child of Loki instead by the time I hit puberty. He's the trickster, a god of mischief and trouble, and it sure seemed like he was really my father."

She paused there, evidently lost in her memories. After a moment of star-gazing she resumed. "Things started happening around me. A girl at school who thought she was better than the rest of us tried to make me give up my seat at the lunch table one day and I got mad at her. I didn't hit her or anything, but she fell to the floor holding her head and screaming. Someone else played a harmless practical joke on me and I took offense at it - you know how girls are. Well, she didn't come to school the next day, and we found out that she lost all her memory.

"After a few more incidents like that people couldn't help but notice the connection to me. I was the reason my parents and I were forced to leave the planet. 'Lokisdotter' was known all over the world and welcome nowhere.

"We tried to settle in on different worlds a few times, but before long at each place something else would happen and we'd move again. The money my parents had saved up all their lives was running out and I knew it was all my fault. I didn't know why bad things happened to people that made me mad, but there was no denying it was me doing it somehow. I'd never heard of the psi-corp back then; you know how secretive they are. So to keep my parents from having to keep hiding me - and slowly killing themselves in the process - I left. I was sixteen then, and we had been living on Forsythe. I don't know how much you know about that planet, but it's one of the older worlds and pretty populous. I disappeared into the underbelly of one of the largest cities and never saw my parents again.

Another pause. "I found out later that they spent every last credit they had searching for me. Then first mam and then da died of broken hearts."

I sensed that she needed for me to say something then. "That's awful, but you couldn't have known it would turn out like that. It sounds to me like you left them to spare them any more heartache."

"But I did know, that's just it. They stuck with me no matter what happened. They gave up everything they had to try and give me a good childhood. They could have turned me over to some Imperial agency or other at any time, but they didn't. I killed them, Edj. Nothing you can say will change that."

She was right, of course, and I didn't even try. I just left it there, wishing we weren't stuck in space suits, hiding on an enemy base. I could imagine tears collecting at the corners of her eyes, pooling there with no gravity to make them run, and I desperately wanted to be able to gently wipe them away.

It was several minutes later when she finally spoke again, and it was as if the last part of our conversation hadn't taken place. "So I lived on the streets, mostly by selling what a young girl's got that everyone else wants, until I was just a few weeks over 18. I got picked up by the police as what they called a 'person of interest' and questioned about the mysterious death of a man who several witnesses said I was with on the night he died. No charges were ever filed, but only because a woman they all believed was from the Imperial government showed up and told them I had actually been an undercover agent working under her."

"From the way you phrased that," I said, "I get the impression she wasn't really who she claimed to be."

I could hear a hint of a grin in her voice as she answered. "You got it. Martha took me in and taught me how to control my abilities. It wasn't easy at first, but eventually a whole new range of possibilities opened up before me."

"Like, oh, selling clandestine protective services, perhaps?"

She actually laughed at that, which was a dramatic improvement over her mood of just a few minutes earlier.

JD couldn't have picked a better time to return. He ran a fiber-optic cable to each of our suits to avoid any detectable signals being given off and patched his recording into both of our visors.

The first thing we saw was that the two large civilian ships both appeared to have been moored in the same place for some time, to judge by the accumulation of dust static-adhering to their hulls. I guessed these to be living quarters for whoever was working here, and Mela agreed after we saw shuttlecraft depart from the hangar bay of one and head into the planetoid's interior.

Next we noticed a circular array of what look like flat sheets of dull gray metal covering an area some 200 yards in diameter. Mela had no idea what this was for, but I recognized it right away. I had, in fact, been expecting to find something like it.

"Think about it," I explained. "Other than the ships flying around, we detected no neutrino emissions. There are no fusion reactors in operation here. Well, except one, anyway."

"What? I thought you just said…"

"One really big one, right in the middle of the system."

"I get it now. That must be a receiver for power being beamed in from collectors closer to the sun."

"I'll make a proper recon expert out of you yet," I told her, and was rewarded with another laugh. Yep, her mood sure had recovered.

It was what we learned of the interior of the shell that surprised me.

Sam had said that inside the planetoid was a metallic construct of some kind. Yeah, and a star is a warm ball of gas that gives off a little light. It was way bigger than any habitat, any station, *any* man-made object I've ever heard of. According to the scale provided by the display, this thing was a sphere a good 200 miles and change in diameter.

Not a solid body, no, but still...

The interior of the planetoid was illuminated by hundreds of bright floodlights anchored all around its inner surface. As to what they made visible, well, I was impressed. There's no denying it, I was truly in awe that something so large could be built, especially in secret and so far from anywhere.

As I said, it wasn't a solid object but rather an open framework composed of probably thousands of interconnected girders. And not just a buckyball shell, either. From what I could tell from the footage, it could be like that all the way to its center. The gaps between the girders would be big enough to fly the *Wah* through, but they were arranged in such a way that they crisscrossed in layers.

The thing would be incredibly strong, built like that. Its composition was of foamed nickel-iron steel woven through with carbon-carbon cables, all of which was readily available in this incredibly rich and vast asteroid disk. In fact, a lot of the raw materials could have come from the core of the very ice ball it was built inside of. Talk about convenient...

Why it needed to be that strong and what all the minzite was for were more questions the scan could not answer. For those, we were going to have to do more than take a few pictures.

Fortunately, I had a good idea of where to start looking for more information. Besides the buckyball, inside the planetoid's shell the ore freighter that had led Sam here was docked with what could be nothing else but the manufacturing ship which had forged all those girders. If you're after construction files, a factory ship's computers aren't a bad place to look.

"That's our target," I told Mela, highlighting it in our displays.

"But how are we going to get to it? Surely they're keeping an eye on all access points. I know I would be, even with all the other security measures they've got going on."

"So would I. That's why we're going to make our own, right here."

At first she didn't understand what I intended. "What do you mean, by blasting our way in? I know you don't. That would be a dead giveaway that we are here. So how?"

I can't blame her for not catching on. After all, she hasn't lived with a tame black hole her whole life. "My good friend Sam is so fastidious that when he eats, not a crumb or stray subatomic particle falls off his plate."

After Sam was done generously ensuring we had a way in, we made the crossing without seeing any sign that we had been detected. I led Mela and JD to a touchdown on the factory ship's hull just outside an airlock that appeared to be only for the use of inspection or repair workers.

"I know you're not going to just walk right in, not after all this other skulking around. What's the plan?"

I'll give her credit. She was catching on.

"Have you ever heard of a computer virus?"

I think she shook her head 'no', but then realized that inside her armor I couldn't see it, because after a second she said, "No, what's a computer virus?"

"Well, in the earliest days of computers, malicious or just fun-loving people could write software that made the primitive machines of the time do things their designers never intended, and often without the user's even knowing about it. Quantum processing, when it was developed, made doing that next to impossible. But guess what?"

"Hmm, let's see. Something tells me that there are ways to still do that, ways known only to those at the very top of the Empire and forbidden for us mere peons to even know about, probably on pain of mindwipe."

"Ha. Pretty much. Only some of the best experts in the field even know that it's possible. And that knowledge has been deliberately suppressed for hundreds of years, but with good reason. Can you imagine the chaos that would result if people realized the computers they trust to do everything from handle their finances to diagnose their illnesses and fly their cars and spacecraft could be taken over by a prankster or worse? Our entire society would be brought to its knees."

"Yeah, I guess so." She sounded thoughtful. I'd given her something profound to think about all right.

Before she could grow too depressed from the knowledge of just how close we perpetually live to the brink of complete societal breakdown, I threw her a bone of hope. "But don't let it bother you too much. Hacking an AI can only be done using another, much more sophisticated AI running on a platform an order of magnitude faster than the best commercially available system. By law, these highest-end computers are rigidly regulated and only run under constant supervision, even though only the military can even legally possess them."

"And the Prince, right?"

"Hey, hey, what can I do? What good is having all these super-duper ultra-secret gadgets if I don't ever get the opportunity to put them to good use?"

And I did. The penetrator AI, code-named 'Backtrack' after an ancient hacker's favorite software package, was actually run on a dedicated computer hidden deep within my ship - the only one such in the Empire not under direct military control. Being the prince has its advantages, as I believe I've said.

To be effective, though, it needs to be able to interface with its victim computer. That's where another nifty and incredibly expensive little gadget comes in handy. Since many situations where I might need to employ Backtrack are of a clandestine nature where using standard RF comms could lead to discovery, the technical wizards that had supplied me with so many of my best tools had included a short-range ansible to link the AI to a handheld multimode interface module. Not only is this communication undetectable, it is also instantaneous, which is vitally important to Backtrack's operation since even the tiniest time lag could lead to its failure to overcome another AI's defenses.

Sorry if I digress; computer systems, both past and present, have always interested me. And the Royal archivists who asked for these accounts did tell me to include anything I feel might help future readers understand what influence the decisions that led to the fall of the Old Empire and the Dark Age that followed.

So anyway, I briefly explained all this to Mela as I held the MMIM - multimode interface module - up to the airlock's exterior control panel. Within seconds it had done its job and the wide outer door slid open.

"That's one handy lockpick you've got there," she said with what I could tell was a touch of envy. "But why do we have to go aboard at all if it can access the ship's computers from here? Can't you just tell it to find the files we need and then we can get back to the ship?"

"I wish it was that easy, but no. Remember what I just said about signal lag? What that means is that the farther away we are from what I'm trying to access or control, the greater chance there is that Backtrack will be detected. So to get a door to open without reporting that it did, it's best to be right at the door control. Same way with file storage - we need to find either the central data storage nexus of this ship or the actual construction machines that built the components of that... thing out there."

By the time I explained this the airlock had cycled and we were granted access to the interior of the factory ship. As I had expected, the area we emerged into was an out-of-the-way corridor lined with storage rooms containing spare parts and tools for the repair of external equipment.

The first thing I needed to find was a computer terminal, which I located just inside the larger of the two parts storerooms. After JD followed Mela and me in and the automatic sliding doors closed behind us, I once again interfaced Backtrack into the ship's system.

This time I had access to much more than a mere airlock's controls. First, I downloaded a schematic of the entire ship from public-access general data and piped it into both of our suits. This was perfectly safe, but I still instructed my AI to erase the log recording at this, not wanting anyone to notice it and wonder why the ship's layout was pulled from such an unlikely terminal.

What I did next was far riskier, but something vital to our success. I had Backtrack gain access to the ship's internal sensors and erase any traces of us as they were received, as well as pass along to our suits the location of everyone aboard. This was possible because it was able to inject this data as a hidden signal mixed in with the myriad other bits of information disseminated by the shipwide wireless network. Our suits, of course, were told precisely how to uncover this critical intelligence. There was a definite chance that either a technician or an AI would notice this addition, but it would take time to decode what the extra signal was for; more time, I hoped, then we would be aboard.

With the map of the ship and its inhabitants showing up as a semi-transparent overlay in our visors, we were ready to head out. Masked from internal sensors and practically invisible to anyone who might otherwise see us with their primary biological visual sensors - except for Mela's right calf, anyway - we were as ready as we could be to make our way deeper into the outlaw ship.

I thought I'd thought of everything.

CHAPTER 7

The factory ship didn't have a name, unless you counted its designation, AF-28-B6, as one. It also didn't have - or require - much in the way of a crew. This was mostly composed of maintenance engineers, there to keep everything running smoothly. They were either clustered around the living quarters - those that were off-duty, presumably - or spread out amongst the various production bays, according to our personnel locator.

This made my decision of where to start looking for clues an easy one, for no one was near the ship's computer core. We made our way through deserted corridors with almost contemptible ease, never even coming close to anyone. At one point Mela asked, "Why are there so few people aboard?"

To which I replied, "Well, this is an automated factory ship, you know. And besides, it looks like the biggest part of the construction project is over and done with."

"It feels like it's too easy, us just walking the halls like this. Especially after all the sneaking around it took just to get us here."

"Sometimes it's like that, and I, for one, am just as glad it is."

And so it was that we gained access to a terminal right outside the main data store itself with no one seeing - or otherwise detecting - us at all. And it was there that we experienced our first major disappointment.

There were no files left that had anything to do with the big sphere.

Oh, sure, there were generic instructions for how to produce

things like girders and superconducting cable and shield generators, but nothing to indicate how the components were to be as-
sembled, much less the ultimate purpose of it all.

We were there a good half hour, and the most I could tease
out of the computer was a total of how many of each item had
been built. This only raised more questions, though. Why did
they need so many shielding nodes? Or so many anti-gravity minz
coils, for that matter?

"If you promise not to say I told you so, I'll let you in on a little
secret," I told Mela when I'd gotten all I could from the computer.

With a laugh, she said, "It's a deal. What's your secret?"

"I'm glad you talked me into letting you come, because now
it's your turn to find us some intel."

"So, Mister I've Got It Handled needs my help? Wow? Who
could have known?"

What I was asking was illegal in normal circumstances, and
for good reason. Any official use of psionics is highly regulated,
mainly because there is no defense against it that doesn't involve
the use of powerful and dangerous drugs.

On the other hand, it was nothing that Mela hadn't been doing
all her adult life. And I am the prince, after all. My authority is second only to my father's.

"But not just anybody," I told her with an exaggerated nod,
which was more like a bow in the armor suits. "We need to find
someone who's likely to know more than the average technician."

"And it would be much better if we can catch him alone," she
added.

When she said that I first thought she was being cute, because
of course it would be better - and safer - to take someone who was
by himself. But then she went on to prove how little I actually
knew about the abilities of a powerful psionic.

"That way I can make him forget he was ever questioned."

Oh, man, did the implications of that simple statement ever
shake the foundation of my sanity. Had something like that ever
happened to me? Would I ever know it? I decided I would need
to have a long talk with certain experts next time I made it to

Alphum.

With no way to tell who was who among the dots on our map, we had to take a look at where the individual crewmen were to try to determine who was most likely to be our best informant. We finally settled on one working in what was listed as the 'proto-typing lab'. While it was possible he or she was nothing more than a low-level tech doing nothing more than performing routine maintenance on the equipment there, it was more likely to be someone with sufficient seniority to know what that big ball outside was intended to do.

That, and he also met our other requirement of being there by himself.

We once again took to the abandoned corridors and made our stealthy way through the ship. Mela stopped me in the passageway just outside the room where our target worked, oblivious to our presence. "This is close enough. I can sense him from here."

"But don't we need to question him? If he isn't thinking about what we need can you still get it out of him?"

"I probably could, but it would leave him a wreck. No, to do this without leaving any evidence, the first step is to put him to sleep before he sees us."

Okay, I'll admit it - I was way out of my depth. "Then, by all means, proceed."

She already had. "That's done. Now we can go in."

What we found in the lab was a man of late middle-age, probably somewhere in his early 200s, although with people on any decent brand of longevity regimen it's hard to really tell. He had the faintly-lined face and finely textured skin of someone who had stabilized his age long ago, but his soft limbs bore the extra flesh of someone once very muscular but who has long since lost his strength with the decline in physical activity brought on by time itself. His hair, too, spoke of a long life by its spider-silk fineness, an unmistakable sign of advancing years. And then there were the telltale lumps on his temples where a truly antique pair of cerebral-boost implants lay just under the skin.

He was sitting on a stool, slumped over on a worktable littered with the tools and partially-assembled inner workings of multiple machines, the hallmark of tinkerers everywhere. While not snoring, it was plain that he was, indeed, sound asleep.

"Amazing. You can do that to anyone?"

"Not really. It helps that he was calm and not expecting anything. Is it safe for us to open our visors?"

My integrated combat systems hadn't detected any obvious security cameras, but that didn't mean there weren't any there. On the other hand, there didn't seem to be any logical reason for there to be any visual sensors in the lab, either. "I suppose so, if there's a good reason. Why?"

"In the mental state I'm going to put him in he'll be very easily disoriented. Being able to see our faces will help him to focus on us and our questions."

"And he won't remember any of this?"

"That I can guarantee. I've had a lot of practice with this."

A shudder went through me at that admission. I really didn't want to dwell on the thoughts that it brought up, so I quickly told her, "Go ahead, then."

A minute later the old engineer sat up, but he did not appear to be awake. He didn't look around, nor did he make any other movements. His eyes just stared blankly straight ahead. Mela hadn't said a word, but I knew she was responsible for his state.

Following her lead, I stepped around his workbench to a point directly in front of him and raised my helmet visor. "Can you hear me?" I asked.

His voice was flat, uninflected. "Yes."

"What do you know about the big buckyball you people are building?"

When he just sat there staring at me without so much as blinking an eye, much less answering, Mela said, "You'll have to be a lot more specific. He can answer direct questions but not anything that involves much reasoning or speculation."

"Okay, let's try this again. What is the ultimate purpose of the large construct being built outside?"

"I am unaware of its ultimate purpose."

I could tell this was going to be fun. From the basics, then. "What is the construct called?"

"It is referred to as D.I.S.K., or 'DISK'."

"That's an acronym. What does it stand for?

"I don't know."

"And what powers this DISK?" Maybe I could still work out something of its purpose by learning more about it.

"An antimatter reactor at its core."

"Whoa, that's serious power," I said.

Mela cocked an eyebrow at me which I assumed was an invitation to explain.

"An antimatter reactor liberates orders of magnitude more energy than nuclear fusion, but it is much more difficult to contain the reaction. The only practical way to do so is to employ enormously powerful force fields arrayed in a sphere all around it. So if the DISK was hollow at its core, lined with field generators... Hmm, that could explain why it needs to be built so strong, to resist the enormous pressure. But I can't imagine it needing but a fraction of the number of force-field nodes that were built. What are the rest of them for?"

"To keep it from being shot down?"

"It still doesn't add up. With that much power available, a tenth as many could produce a shield strong enough to hold off a fleet of warships. Whatever this thing is, somebody expects it to stand up to anything that can be thrown against it."

"So, it's some kind of weapon."

"Maybe not. It's certainly not any kind of planet-killer design I've ever heard about." For the first time since I'd learned about this whole situation, the thought occurred to me that it might not be about building a weapon.

"Okay, then what the heck is it?"

"Well, I'm starting to wonder if this DISK isn't intended to survive in a high-pressure environment, like deep inside a gas giant planet."

"You're losing me."

"Give me a minute." I turned it back to our captive engineer.

"You! What has all the minzite being used for? Anti-gravity or lo-calized gravity coils?"

With the same expressionless tone he'd been using, he said, "Anti-gravity."

I turned back to Mela. "Yeah, it makes sense. The structural strength to reinforce the inner tension-field generators around the antimatter reactor, more shield nodes and inward-facing anti-gravity coils all around the perimeter, something like this could be used to, oh, I don't know, maybe mine exotic materials from the hearts of supergiant planets."

I wasn't the only one becoming convinced by my deductions, either, as Mela jumped in. "And that stuff would probably sell for incredible prices, right? So all this could be just nothing more than a big-money project? That makes more sense than someone spending all this money to build a weapon."

"Yeah. I'll still have to confirm it all, though. But I think we're done with this guy."

"Alright. Let's step back into the hall and I'll take care of him."

When that was done she asked me where we were going next. When I told her she laughed and said, "Why not? It's what we came here to look at, after all."

The DISK looked incredibly huge from a distance of 100 miles away. From a couple of hundred yards, it was hard to believe that it was really that big. The difference was that, from far out, you could see what looked like a small moon made up of black spider webbing, but up close all you saw was an infinitely-deep layer of 20-ft wide cylindrical beams, a porous mass whose extent it was impossible to gauge so you naturally assumed it was only slightly larger than your eyes could encompass.

On its outermost layer, every junction of these struts met in flat round plates a hundred feet in diameter. One of these was my first target for investigation. I had Sam tow us to the opposite side of the DISK from the opening in the planetoid and the factory ship, since only there did I feel comfortable taking active scans with my probing tools.

The scans confirmed what I'd suspected about superconducting cables feeding power to a crazy number of shield generator nodes, and also to an equally insane amount of minz coils. Well, that explained where all the minzite had gone, but not why. Oddly, the coils were almost all positioned facing *outward*, which made no sense at all.

"I'll be the first to admit," I confided in Mela, "that I'm no expert engineer. But at least it still doesn't look like any kind of weapon. It'll be interesting to see what the eggheads back home make of all the scans." Next, I adjusted for a wider, more inclusive look into the huge structure. It did indeed have a large hollow at its center, which fit with the claim of it being antimatter powered. This scan also showed something else I'd expected to find but had come across no mention of yet: engines.

Colossal amounts of power would be required to nullify the mass of something this large and to drive it through space, but again, that was not a problem for the DISK's designers. And while precisely coordinating the operation of a dozen hyperdrive motivators would be challenging, apparently they thought they had that worked out, too.

When completed, the DISK device, whatever its purpose, would be able to get itself there.

And that completion date could not be far off.

On our flight around the huge sphere I noticed that many of the junction plates still had gaps in them, which I now knew were waiting to be filled with minz coils. Coils to be made from the minzite ore I'd brought, most likely, I thought wryly.

I also had to assume that whatever mining or surveying equipment that was to be included in its final loadout had yet to be installed, for there was no trace of anything like that yet.

There wasn't anything resembling a crew compartment, but that didn't really surprise me. Something intended for any environment this baby was built for would probably be unmanned, operated by an AI that could be an ansible contact with anywhere.

Mela had been quiet while I took my readings and explained to them to her, but when she saw me stowing the multiscanner she asked, "So what's the verdict?"

"The jury is still out. I think the best thing for us to do is get back to the *Wah*, send everything we've collected to the experts, and wait for them to decide what this really is. At the least, I'd expect the navy to show up here in force to make them answer for the crime of minzite smuggling. What they can do about someone building a new kind of mining ship way out here beyond the borders of the Empire, I don't know."

"Don't you want to know who's behind all this?"

"Of course I do, but there was nothing in the factory ship's computer..."

"That's not the only ship here, now is it?"

I can't say that I hadn't thought the same thing, but I'd dismissed it as not being worth the risk. If I'd been by myself, maybe, but not with Mela to think about.

"It's too dangerous and wouldn't gain us anything that won't come out eventually anyway."

"That's *if* there's still anyone here when the navy arrives. You said yourself that this thing is too close to being finished. Come on, you know I'm right. If we don't try to learn who's doing this you may never know."

It wasn't the first time I've ever let a woman talk me into doing something against my better judgment, and it probably won't be the last, either.

CHAPTER 8

I decided to split us up. While there was much to potentially be learned by boarding the passenger ship, the DISK's computers themselves undoubtedly held many answers as well. So, to make the best use of our individual strengths, I gave JD the ansible-equipped MMIM and sent him to the DISK while Mela and I snuck in on the tail of one of the shuttles returning to the passenger ships, literally. We affixed ourselves magnetically to the aft section of one that we happened to catch just departing the factory ship and went along for the ride.

It should have gotten us into a hangar undetected. It would have, I'm sure, if they hadn't been looking for us.

That they were was obvious, but by the time they acted it was too late for us to get away. They let the shuttle in as usual, routing it through the hanger's force field into a berth at the inner end of a row of similar shuttles. So far so good. I thought we had made it.

Then the jaws of the trap sprang shut.

Space armor, especially the top-end models like Mela and I wore, can soak up a lot of punishment. I've heard accounts of guys wearing similar models surviving assaults by entire battalions of enemy soldiers armed with weapons that could take out a starfighter.

It is made to resist all sorts of toxic and corrosive atmospheres and liquids and is servo-boosted to both strengthen its wear and enable him to function in moderately high gravity. Air and water recyclers, a supply of food concentrate, and a nuclear-decay power source mean that it can be worn for over a week if necessary.

It's great stuff, this armor. It isn't perfect, though, but what is? One failing that is common to all personal armor is that a sufficiently strong force field projected from enough points surrounding it can immobilize it, leaving the wearer trapped like a bug in amber.

And that's exactly what they did to us. The instant the shuttle came to a halt, the hangar bay's accident-containment thick field came on at full intensity. Suddenly even my servo-boosted strength wasn't enough to so much as let me raise my middle finger to my captors.

They kept us pinned like that for over an hour. We could breathe, of course, and otherwise wiggle around within the confines of our suits. Obviously our captors wanted us alive. They also wanted to soften us up, mentally. I'm proud to say that the Tarkle line is made of sterner stuff than most, and it would take significantly more than an hour's immobilization to even begin to force the first crack in my psyche.

Mela freaked out. Her claustrophobia, barely under control as it was, hit her with all the force of a star going nova. She screamed, she whimpered, she cried, she hyperventilated, and there was nothing whatsoever I could do for her. She was beyond hearing anything I could say to try and calm her down.

During all this, business went on as usual in the hanger. The passengers departed from the shuttle we were stuck to, and later another vessel up the line from us was loaded and took off. Service robots went about their duties, and no one paid us much attention.

Mela had finally subsided into a fugue state of shallow breathing punctuated by the occasional whimper. She'd been that way for a good third of an hour when at last I saw something happening that was obviously related to us.

A military transport, apparently from one of the patrolling warships, entered the hanger.

"Come on, Melanada, snap out of it! Our official welcoming committee is finally here. Hey! Wake up! Are you with me?"

I could hear her taking some deep breaths and getting herself settled. "Alright, alright, I'm with you."

What it looked like was that they were preparing to take us down, anyway. A full fifty-man squad had filed out of the military shuttle and taken up stations all around us. Some thirty of them were arrayed in a semicircle on the deck facing us, each one holding a heavy weapon of one sort or another. The rest had spread out in pairs to occupy vantage points elsewhere, some on the upper mezzanine level of the hangar and others on top of several of the nearer shuttles. And as a final show of respect, their transport itself deployed a weapons turret and trained its anti-ship blasters on us.

Their uniforms weren't familiar to me, but that was not surprising. They were most likely from one of the many mercenary outfits from the Empire's neighboring Aligarth Hegemony, which is absolutely full of them. They seemed professional and well-disciplined, though, which is what counts. We wouldn't catch any breaks due to any lack of ability on their part.

When everyone was in position their commander stepped forward a few paces closer to us than the rest of his line. He was a trim, fit man who moved with the poise and grace of a consummate martial artist. His crisp, clean uniform was devoid of any rank insignia, as is common practice among the mercs who did not want to advertise who is a prime target, but it was clear to me that he was their leader. Maybe it had something to do with the fact that he was the only one not wearing armor, I don't know.

He was wearing - or was implanted with, more likely - a comm set, though, for his voice came through on the general talk band that my suit was tuned to monitor. He got right to the point, too. "You have been captured while performing an illegal reconnaissance in privately-held space and aboard private property. In accordance with the Taráned Document I am hereby offering you the choice of surrendering yourselves to face impartial judgment or fighting for your freedom. How do you choose?"

Like I really had a choice. If I'd been by myself, it would have been different, but with Mela to think about...

She was in no shape to fight, even if she'd been fully trained and experienced in armored combat. And while the ancient Taráned Document is supposed to give any soldier caught in enemy territory a fighting chance at escape, the deck was clearly stacked against us. Fifty soldiers and a combat shuttle against us too, and outside, I'm sure both warships awaited their chance at us as well.

Besides, we were there to learn everything we could about these people. And we didn't have to *stay* prisoners, after all. I gave the traditional reply. "In accordance with the Taráned Document, I offer our parole while admitting to nothing."

After switching back to our private channel, I told Mela, "Let's just go along with them for now and learn all we can. They won't hurt us as long as we act civil. Don't try to hide the truth, either. If they catch you in a lie they're liable to make it that much worse. And don't worry, I'll get us free when the time is right."

In short order, we were relieved of our armor right there in the hangar. Wearing only shorts and t-shirts, the standard under-armor dress, we were led at gunpoint to separate cells in the passenger ship's brig. Mela look relieved at the last time I saw her. I suppose after being in armor for so long, and the last hour immobilized armor at that, even captivity was good if it got her out of it.

The expected questioning came about as soon as I thought it would, after just long enough for them to have examined our armor. The door to my cell opened and in stepped an armed and armored merc who took up a position of watchfulness in the corner. Following him was the commander who had taken our surrender and another merc, this one almost a carbon copy of his superior and acting like a second-in-command or aide-de-camp.

Again the leader proved he was not one for small talk. Without introducing himself he launched right into the interrogation. "That's high-grade armor you were wearing. Who are you and who do you represent?"

I had been sitting on the edge of the single bunk and hadn't risen when my interrogator came in, but I did so before answering his question. In my proudest regal posture of attention, I informed him who I am.

I'd no more than gotten "Prince Edj" out of my mouth when I saw the number-two man swallow nervously. By the time I finished my title, even the commander was looking like he wished he was elsewhere. I do have a certain reputation as someone who is more than capable of defending myself. I finished by demanding to know who I was addressing.

He maintained his poise, I'll say that for him. "I am General Atticus Palermo, commander of the Free Company of Legionnaires." He snapped a crisp salute to me, then turned his head to address his subordinate. "Inform Lord D'Orneo who our guest is and that I request his presence immediately."

Number Two stomped his right heel, saluted his leader with a fist to his breast, and left without a word.

I barely paid him any attention, because suddenly nearly everything made sense. 'Lord' Lumar D'Orneo was a name known throughout the Empire. Formerly the Lord Governor of the world of Villalba, a planet known for its many resorts, casinos, theme parks and other attractions, he famously fled the Empire six years ago with his family and closest cronies when it was discovered that he had embezzled trillions of credits from the planetary economy during his tenure there. The vast majority of the money had never been recovered, for he had prudently, and secretly, invested in all sorts of hard wealth such as art, jewels and starships, and moved them out of the Empire over the course of years. It was the single biggest theft in Imperial history, and he had the distinction of being the number-one most wanted criminal in the Ninety-Nine.

Financing the construction of the DISK, including buying all of the minzite it required, would hardly put a dent in his enormous wealth. Unfortunately, the chances of him building it as a benign exploratory or mining ship were just about zero. Anything he was involved in could have but one objective: to make good the threat he broadcast throughout the Empire as he took his leave of us: to kill all members of the House of Tarkle and claim the Empire as his own.

"Allow me to make one thing very clear to you, Your Highness," General Palermo said. "Neither I, personally, nor the Free Legionnaires as a company have any ill intentions toward you or the Empire. However, I am honor-bound by my sworn contract to defend Lord D'Orneo and obey all directives given me by him. In the event this places me or anyone under my command in the position of having to employ force against your person I would ask that you remember this and correctly assign responsibility where it belongs."

In other words, he was trying to cover his own backside in case I came out ahead. As I said, my reputation precedes me. Unfortunately for him, he hadn't paid enough attention to the part about me holding every man responsible for his own actions.

"And I want you to understand something, too. If you choose to act on any order that urges you to commit immoral or treasonous acts, no degree of chain-of-command blame-dodging can absolve you of your own responsibilities. Do I make myself clear?"

He just stood there unmoving, staring at a spot over my shoulder, while I bore into his eyes with all of the righteous dignity that a thousand years of Imperial ancestry had bred into me.

We were still like that when his aide returned a minute later. In perfect form, the man saluted and said, "Sir, the Lord D'Orneo asks you to escort His Highness to the midships observation blister, where he will join you shortly."

The journey through the ship was like a progression through social classes on a rigidly stratified world. The brig and its immediate surroundings were all cold functionality with no energy spent on anything beyond mere survival. Next came utilitarian corridors that, although they led to infrastructure access, at least had been painted in pleasant, matching colors. Farther on there were areas encompassing both living and entertainment venues, while at both the literal and figurative top, beauty and comfort met luxury and idleness in the opulence of a chamber devoted to stargazing by the haughtiest of all. The general, his aide, and I were followed by a light guard of four soldiers with weapons drawn. I had given my word not to attempt to escape so long as I was treated fairly, but that was before I learned that I was in the domain of the man who wanted to eradicate my family and all we stand for. When we entered the hemispherical observation blister, these four spread out to the four directions and stood at the ready along the circumference of the dome.

The room itself was furnished in a style that might be called mega-rich extravagance. Everywhere were shelves and pedestals displaying priceless art and artifacts. Reclining loungers upholstered in the rarest leathers had smoky Orion-wood side tables trimmed in rainbow-hued s'laar-bone beside them. Elsewhere was a 20-ft wide bed of living dornu flesh scattered with Earth-silk pillows, just waiting to psychically enhance the tactile sensations of any couples or groups who might lay, or play, on it. The very floor itself was carpeted in sweet-smelling, mildly-euphoric evergrass. You get the idea. It was the kind of place that would remind D'Orneo of the luxuries he'd lived amongst for so many years. I imagine he spent a lot of time there.

Personally, I was more taken by the view through the transparent dome. Millions of asteroids of all sizes, colors and compositions filled the sky in a slow dance against a backdrop split vertically between unfiltered stars and the empty blackness of Intergalactic space. It was the kind of view that made a contemplative person reflect on his place among all that the universe contains.

We had been there no more than two minutes before my appreciation of the glories of the cosmos was rudely interrupted by the arrival of that paragon of arrogant narcissism himself, the former Lord Lumar D'Orneo.

Decked out in a costume that would have embarrassed any self-respecting circus clown, he was the epitome of deluded fashion blindness. There must have been two dozen bright, clashing colors among his puffy pants, curly-toed slippers, wide sash belt, balloon-armed pleated shirt, and lopsided beret cap. It's been said that he fancies himself an artist and trendsetter, but I don't know of anyone who has actually copied his flamboyant dress for anything other than a joke. Perhaps among a certain set on Villalba there were some who took him seriously back in his day, but if so they would never admit to it now.

His body, and especially his face, had been tweaked into the idea of physical perfection. He was neither too tall nor too short, too thin or too muscular. His facial features were based on mathematical models that supposedly describe the ideal masculine form: firm chin, full but not over-full lips, strong slightly-arched nose, protruding but not angular cheekbones, large brown eyes, and medium-weight eyebrows. His hair, what there was of it not covered by his cap, was short, tightly curled and a golden blond, which almost completely matched his skin complexion. He was known to be at least 130 years old but looked 25.

Did I mention that he was a narcissist? He came in accompanied by a black-jumpsuited servant who carried a 2-ft tall mirror and was constantly trying to keep it in his master's line-of-sight, dancing this way in that whenever D'Orneo shifted his head. I couldn't help but wonder if the poor fellow was on some kind of punishment detail.

The former governor's manner was as extroverted as his outfit. He habitually talked loudly, using his hands in wide, extravagant gestures, and was never still. When he made his entrance he immediately started talking as he approached the mercs and me. "Oh my, oh my! What an absolutely wonderful surprise!" He clapped his hands grandly, as happy as a child at a surprise birthday party.

"Oh, my dear Prince Edj! It has been an unforgivably long time since I've seen you! What have you been doing with yourself? How are the royal mum and pop? Did you know that I was planning on paying a visit to Alphum soon? I am, oh yes!" Clap, clap, clap.

It was almost comical watching the poor servant struggle to keep up as D'Orneo swept into the middle of the chamber and then shifted this way and that as he babbled on at breakneck speed.

"You simply must tell me what brings you here to our little party! What in the cosmos is the heir of the throne of the Ninety-Nine Stars doing out here in the nether regions? Out for a little love cruise with your girlfriend? What would mum and pop say? Oh you cheeky little prince. What are we going to do with you?"

To someone who didn't know any better, the megalomaniac before me might have been taken as somewhat eccentric but basically harmless. I knew better. All his foolishness aside, Lumar D'Orneo is a cold, ruthless tyrant who has no empathy whatsoever for his fellow man. Any seeming cordiality is just a mask over the heartless face of a remorseless, sadistic maniac who will stop at nothing to bring ruin to my family and the Empire we serve.

I didn't want to even be in the same quadrant with him, much less speak to him, but not only would I have to do that, but I'd also have to be careful not to provoke him into one of his famous rages. I had Mela to think about, and she was his helpless prisoner.

"I was in the neighborhood and I heard someone was buying up a lot of minzite without tipping the government its due, so I thought I'd drop by and see why someone would do such a thing."

"Oh, isn't that just like you, little prince, always off trying to find rights to wrong or whatever! You are so gallant. The very embodiment of noble virtue. The peasants of the empire are so fortunate to have one such as yourself looking out for them. If only they knew how despicable the Tarkles truly are. I wonder what they'd say then."

Holding my tongue was not easy, but I knew this was not the time to take him on. His day would come, I kept telling myself.

"So tell me, oh do, what do you think of my new little toy?"

"What 'toy' would that be?" I asked dryly, although I knew good and well what he was talking about.

"Oh, don't be coy, dear princeling. I know you asked one of my little wire-heads all about it."

Suddenly I knew exactly how they'd been tipped off about our presence. How could I have been so stupid? I couldn't blame Mela, though, for how was she to know that the engineer we'd questioned was implanted with a type of brain-enhancing augment that continuously records everything the user experiences? Those went out of style over a century ago after people finally realized that they didn't really want to relive every boring moment of their lives.

But if someone with one were to realize that a span of time was missing from their memory, it would be trivial for him to find out what really happened. And from there, with the security forces knowing what to look for, we were bound to be detected no matter how stealthy our camouflage. If only we had just gone straight back to the *Wah* like I originally wanted to.

"Oh ho! You didn't know how we discovered you and your latest bed warmer. How delicious! I can practically see your little brain working! Oh my, yes!" He peered intently at the side of my head as if he really could see my thoughts.

I knew he couldn't, though, because if he really had known what I was thinking just then he would have run away and hidden in the deepest hole he could find. I was getting seriously fed up with his whole manner, and while I'm not generally one to contemplate torture, for him I would gladly make an exception. At the moment I was seeing him being skinned alive an inch at a time.

"But what did you really learn from him, hmm? That my DISK is better shielded and has more power available than any other ship in the galaxy. Oh, I do love all that power! But what, you ask, could I want with something so strong?" He turned to the general and his aide. "Guess what he thought the DISK is for? Go ahead, guess."

"I'm sure I have no idea, my Lord."

"Oh, you're no fun! Would you believe he actually thought it was to mine the core of a giant gas ball! Isn't that a hoot? He thought... haha... he really thought..." D'Orneo actually leaned forward and slapped his knees he was laughing so hard. "I can't believe it! And a mining ship! Like I would waste years and billions of credits to do something as droll as drill! Oh my, oh..."

He took his cap off and fanned his face with it for a moment until he noticed his mirror-bearer wasn't keeping up with his rapid movements. His whole demeanor changed in an instant. Gone were the smiles and laughter, replaced by a cold gaze that could almost freeze the heart of a sun.

He laid into the hapless servant in an icy, razor-sharp tone. "You witless imbecile! How hard can it be to do one simple task all day long? But you, you are incapable of following even one command! Didn't I tell you what would happen if you failed me again? Answer me!"

The poor man's terror was plain to see in the haunted, fearful droop of his eyes and the quivering of his mouth. I could tell that he didn't want to have to reply but was even more scared not to. "Y... you said... you said you'd... m... ma... make my bones... into a m... m... mirror stand. Oh, please, Lord, I won't fail you again! Please, give me one more chance to..."

"Silence! I gave you your 'one more chance' already!"

The mirror dropped out of the condemned servant's nerveless fingers and he fell to his knees on the evergrass and buried his face in it, blubbering, "Mercy, Lord," over and over.

D'Orneo didn't know the meaning of mercy, though, as tale after tale from his days as the ruler of Villalba attested to. But as bad as he treated those who displeased him back then, he had still been under the Empire's laws. Out here, far into unclaimed space, he'd become a law unto himself and nothing was beyond his sadistic streak.

"General! Have this pathetic mongrel taken to Zilhaus immediately. I want the long bones of his arms and legs and every other rib removed and polished. Tell the doctor he is to make sure this wretch is awake and watching the whole time, but he is to use no anesthetic at all! Afterward, I want this waste of amino acids to be fed to my glow-ant colony, but the doctor is to ensure that he lives at least a week!"

General Palermo swallowed his bile and shot a darting worried glance at me as he turned to his aide. "See to it."

That was too much for me. Outside the Empire or not, no one will ever be able to say that prince Edj Tarkle failed to come to the defense of the innocent or needy. Standing there unarmed, wearing nothing but my underwear, practically alone on a ship owned by my arch-nemesis that was protected by two warships full of highly trained mercenaries, weeks of hyper flight beyond the farthest border of the Empire, I took a stand. In my best authoritative, commanding voice I said, "You will do no such thing." To Sam I said, (Be ready.)

To which he replied, (((I am always ready to protect you, Sire.))

I couldn't have shocked anyone any more if I'd pulled a flash-bang grenade out of my shorts and set it off in the middle of the room. Everyone, from the stunned servant still on the floor to the guards ringing the perimeter of the room, looked at me in total and complete amazement. I honestly didn't know what, exactly, I was going to do, but I knew I had to act immediately or it would be too late for the madman's latest victim.

D'Orneo was the first one to recover. He closed his mouth, which had opened wide in surprise at my challenge, looked from the two merc leaders to me, then laughed and said, "Mind your manners, boy. This is my little empire out here and I will do as I please, without you or anyone else interfering in my business. This peon displeased me and he will be punished, just as your father will for what he did to me. As Emperor, he is responsible for the actions of all those under him, so it is only right that everyone in the entire capitol system pay for his actions." His voice took on a maniacal, superior tone as he shouted, "When D'Orneo's Instantaneous Star Killer arrives in the heart of the sun Primax!"

The last piece of the puzzle clicked into place with that announcement. The outward-facing minz coils on the weapon were there to destabilize a star's gravity. It would take only an instant, I realized in a flash. The DISK would exit hyperspace directly in the heart of the target sun. Even its incredibly powerful shields and structural integrity wouldn't protect it for long in such a nuclear furnace, but they wouldn't have to. A star's core is under enormous pressure, and it is only the gravity of its fabulous mass that keeps it contained. Interrupt this gravitational containment for even a fraction of a second and all its hellish fury will be released. Instant supernova! Everything in that star system is vaporized as the explosion sweeps outward in all directions at nearly the speed of light.

And, as if all that wasn't bad enough, the DISK that triggered it will be the only survivor of the cataclysm, since it will have undoubtedly kept its hyper-motivators energized and bounced back into hyperspace on the energy of the star's very destruction, ready to visit the same horror on system after system.

(Quick, Sam, tell Mela what's happening and to…)

((I'm sorry, Sire, but she's not responding.))

Now what? Of course! D'Orneo knew she's a psionic. He would have had her drugged into unconsciousness.

I actually had time to ask myself what else could go wrong. It didn't mean that I wanted a demonstration, but that was what I got.

Apparently on a command from one of D'Orneo's implants, a stasis field just like the one that had trapped us in the hangar bay sprung up around me. I could breathe, but just barely. Any other movement was out of the question. I couldn't believe I was caught the same way twice. I will never, ever, go into a dangerous situation with a woman again!

The Clown of Villalba, as he used to be called by those who did not like or fear him, was once again all smiles and boisterousness. He clapped his hands several times and said, "Stuck again, little prince! And this time it's for good! As much as I would love to keep you around so you can watch the Crystal Palace melt in the nova my DISK will unleash, you are just much too dangerous! Oh my, yes! I know all about your daring escapades and your last-minute escapes from certain death. You see, I know how you and your ancestors have survived every attempt everyone has made to rid this galaxy of the curse of the Tarkles!" He was literally bouncing he was so excited.

"But neither your psionic girlfriend or your little black hole will be able to save you this time! Oh no! Get a good look at the view of the stars from here, because once I open this dome it will be the last thing you ever see! No magic black hole can make you breathe vacuum, Tarkle! A-ha-ha-ha!"

CHAPTER 9

I suppose I shouldn't have been so shocked to hear that he knew about Sam. He had, after all, been a high-ranking government official for years. Longer than I've been alive, as a matter of fact. He'd held several posts before being elected governor, and had served in that capacity for 16 years, and both before and during that time he was frequently seen at court.

His baser tendencies had only come to light in the last few years of his tenure on Villalba, and the investigation my father had instituted concerning him had only started bearing fruit in the couple of months immediately preceding his precipitous departure for parts unknown. What was eventually learned about his misconduct was enough to fuel a highly successful series of immersions and movies as well as a radical cleansing of the upper level of the Villalba planetary government.

And one of the reasons he had been able to hide his nefarious activities for so long, it was discovered, was that he had always made it his business to know as much as he could about the private lives of those who stood in his way. If there were any skeletons in any closets, he not only knew whose bones they were but how and when they'd been interred there.

So no, his knowledge about the Tarkle ace-in-the-hole was not all that far-fetched.

Of course, knowledge can be a double-edged sword. Now that Sam had been outed he was free to act in a much more overt manner. But how? (I could use some encouragement right about now. Any ideas?)

((Don't worry, Sire. I can maintain heat and pressure for you and the respirocytes in your blood will keep you oxygenated more than long enough to reach your vessel.))

That was a relief, let me tell you. While I knew the microscopic artificial red blood cells in my system could let me go ten minutes or more without breathing, I'd had no idea that Sam could do anything to prevent me from freezing solid while suffering fatal decompression injuries. He's just chock-full of surprises.

I just really, really wish he'd told me how he was going to do it. I don't know if we would have been able to come up with an alternative or not, but almost anything would have been better than the way it happened. Again, I'm not blaming Sam. He just doesn't think the same way we do.

△△△

"What's wrong, Edjy? No witty comeback this time?" D'Orneo was positively gloating in his perceived victory.

With Sam's reassurance fresh in my mind I was no longer worried about myself. Mela, though, I still had it to try to save.

"What else is there to say? You outwitted me. I will not sully the Tarkle name by begging for my life. I am curious, though, about your plans for Mela. She's an innocent in all this, you know. She was sent along to keep an eye on me when everyone back on Herrig's thought I was just another smuggler."

"Oh, the girl, the girl! Noble Princie is concerned for the fate of his latest squeeze! Do you mean to tell me you didn't know she's a mindbender?"

I tried to shake my head but couldn't. "I really didn't know, not until she used her parlor trick on me. But she's neither that strong nor talented. It's all she could do to make your technician answer us and look how that turned out!"

"Don't think I don't know what you're doing! She was good

enough to fool the famous Playboy Prince. Oh, have no fear for her. She'll be perfectly safe with me. Why, once I've broken her I'm sure she'll become one of my most valuable assets. I suppose I should thank you for bringing her to me."

My heart sank. Just the thought of what Mela would suffer at the hands of this cruel, heartless monster would have been enough to make me shudder, had I been able to move. I had no doubt he would eventually break her. Anyone can be broken if the person doing the breaking is depraved enough.

(Please, Sam, just this once. D'Orneo is a threat to all Tarkles. Kill him, right now.)

((He is a potential threat. I am not an assassin to be used to kill those whom you merely believe will be a danger at some future time. You know this.))

Sometimes I wonder if I'll ever truly understand him. One minute he'll refuse to kill one person because there's no immediate threat to me, the next he'll kill any number with no hesitation if that's what it takes to save me once that person acts. And he's supposed to exist in all times. What makes him act in one situation and not in another is beyond my grasp. And he has never taken it upon himself to explain the subtleties to me. Inscrutable bastard.

"Well, I'm off. Things to see and people to do and all that. Now, don't you go anywhere, Prince Playboy. Oh no, don't you move. Your little red psi-spy and I are off to see Dr. Zilhaus on my other ship. I think I'll have our shuttle pilot stop right outside this dome on our way over, oh yes! I'll wake her up and give her one last look at you before the good doctor takes her into his care."

With that chilling pronouncement he turned his back on me and started to step away. When he did so he stumbled into the hapless condemned servant who was still sobbing into the slightly narcotic evergrass. With a shriek he danced away, screaming, "You're still here! Just for that, I'll make you feed my glow ants for a month! A month before you can die!"

△△△

Once the vacuum-tight hatch closed and I was alone in the observation blister I had nothing to do but think, and my first thoughts centered on what I wanted to do to D'Orneo once I was free. He would have to be turned over to the Imperial prosecutors to face up to his many, many crimes eventually, but there were some things I wanted to do to him first...

As mildly gratifying as such pleasant ruminations were, I soon realized that I might be wasting precious time. Then it struck me - the evergrass. Its vapor must be filling the air, released by the servants groveling.

(Sam, what can you do about these field generators? I need to get free, now!)

I knew he could see the invisible-to-humans force fields and where they originated, and that it would be a simple matter for him to destroy each emitter node. What I didn't realize was what would happen when one that was fully powered was abruptly taken offline.

It blew out, exploding in a violent burst of white-hot sparks that erupted from the floor almost under my feet.

"Hey! Ouch! Hold on!"

With only one of the many nodes taken out, the restrictive field around me was hardly diminished in strength at all, which was too bad. My left foot had suffered a painful burn, and I couldn't so much as flinch away.

((I'm sorry, Sire. I did not expect that to happen.))

(That's all right. Can you maybe start with the nodes farther away, though?)

That didn't help, either. Apparently they were interconnected in such a way that destroying another one sent a high-energy feedback pulse along the power lines to the previously damaged location. Another shower of sparks shot forth, and with greater violence than before, coming worryingly close to the front of my shorts.

"Whoa, stop! One more like that and there'll never be another generation of Tarkles! Can't you shield me somehow, like what you'll do when the dome goes?"

((I can, but not without causing catastrophic damage to the... Sire, Melanada is telepathically calling your name. She sounds drugged and very weak, psychically.))

I started to ask if he could tell me where she was, but then saw the answer myself. She and that vile snog-eel D'Orneo were standing behind a large window in the front of a shuttlecraft hovering just outside the observation blister's dome. He was going to force her to watch what he thought was going to be my execution, the bastard.

He had one arm around her shoulders and I could see her twitching and trying to pull away. She was having no success, though, probably because of the drugs he was using to suppress her psionics.

"Tell her to hang in there and that I'm coming for her."

((I'm trying, but I do not know if she can hear me.))

Just then I heard an unmistakable Klaxon, the pulse-pounding haunter of every spacer's nightmare, the decompression alarm. And I could see, through the transparent material of the dome, the humid air freezing and crystallizing in space as it was vented from several ports that had opened in its perimeter. A great wind swept up the Earth-silk pillows and every other lightweight item in the room. My ears popped and I opened my mouth, just like everyone is told to do in their emergency training. The volume of the alarm and the whistle of the escaping atmosphere quickly faded out with the loss of pressure, but I felt no other ill effects.

What I did feel, instead, was warmth and a slight increase in air pressure. I realized immediately that I must be inside a bubble of carefully balanced forces of Sam's crafting. It was perfectly spherical and just barely larger in diameter than I am tall, with a sharply defined border like heavily-tinted glass that I could barely see through. It took me but a second longer to realize why this was, for I could see the effect it was having on everything that touched it.

I was *inside* the event horizon of a black hole!

Don't ask me why I wasn't crushed. All I know is that Sam can manipulate the incredible forces that make up his 'body' to a remarkable degree and with pinpoint precision. He makes the most sharply-defined forcefield that human devices can produce look like wispy fog. I was perfectly safe inside, and everything beyond a point a mere inch beyond the event horizon was safe as well, so tight was his control.

But anything that came within that fateful inch of its surface was instantly consumed, somehow bypassing the safe zone I was in and proceeding directly into the all-consuming singularity from which nothing ever emerges. Matter or energy, it makes no difference. Everything is annihilated.

What happened next is another one of those Sam things that I will never understand. When I asked him about it later he just said, ((You were in danger. I needed to convey you to your ship in the quickest manner possible.)) Now, if it had been me driving I would have gone around anything between me and my destination. Apparently a single-minded black hole has no such concerns, however. When one of his charges is in imminent danger nothing else matters to him.

He left a six-foot wide, perfectly round tunnel from the topmost deck of the ship we were on out to a point that exited at an angle some 200 yards and a dozen decks down that, luckily, happened to slice off the end of one of its hyperspace motivators. This same shaft then pierced the planetoid the ship rested on in two places, pointing a straight line to where the *Wah* was hiding among the nearby asteroids.

I was very, very glad that we had left my ship via the cargo airlock and that its large outer door had remained open. Almost as glad as I was that I had the foresight long ago to grow an implant which allowed me to access and control all major ship's systems with a thought so long as I was aboard or within my neuroware's radio range. Closing and pressurizing the airlock would have been problematic otherwise.

I took off for the bridge at a dead run the instant the inner door opened, having already begun bringing all systems up to combat readiness. The time for stealth was long past. Now they were going to get to see what the Crown Prince could bring when he was pissed off.

Even with almost two minutes until the fusion reactor warmed up and stabilized, I still had plenty of power in the storage battery to run everything except the engine and shields. By the time I reached my command post in the center of the bridge I was getting clear returns from all the relevant scanners. Both warships were indeed on station, having been called in during the hour after we'd first been captured, as I'd predicted.

I was also getting readings from the damaged liner. Emergency containment fields had kicked in almost instantly, keeping air and life loss to a minimum. At least that much was in their favor. I hated being responsible for any innocent casualties, even indirectly.

And while the stricken ship wasn't going anywhere, neutrino readings indicated that every other vessel was powering up, including the DISK's antimatter reactor.

"Quick, Sam! Give me a boost toward the planetoid." I then called JD, telling him what had happened and to get off the DISK as quickly as possible.

It was nice not having to wait for fusion power to come online to get moving, because I really couldn't afford to lose any time at all. There was too much to do and very little time in which to do it.

D'Orneo's fleet was preparing to pull out and I had to stop that from happening. But to do that I would have to evade two merc warships and all their efforts to stop me.

And then it got much worse. Before I had covered half the distance to my targets, the mercs launch a dozen TA-2 starfighters. The Tattoo is by far the most common starfighter in all of human space, and with good reason. Fast, agile, capable of carrying a huge amount of ordinance in any imaginable loadout, well armored, easy to maintain and capable of keeping a pilot alive for weeks if necessary, everybody loves it, from the top brass down to the fleet mechanics.

Even a single one is more than the equal of an old freighter like the *Wah*.

Four of them headed my direction, while the rest split themselves evenly between D'Orneo's liner and DISK. These last four dropped off my screen as they entered the planetoid, but even so, I didn't like how the odds were stacked against me at all.

The *Wah's* power plant finally finished its startup sequence just in time for me to get my shields up to full power as the nearest Tattoos got within weapons range. They let loose with a full spread of both missiles and blasters, but between Sam and the shields, nothing of this first volley got through.

If the pilots were surprised that I'd survived this onslaught, it didn't show in their actions. Their course had brought them straight at me, that being the fastest way to intercept an incoming hostile. This meant that they could get off the one barrage as we swept past each other. Even as they went shooting past, though, their pilots were pushing their inertial compensators to the limit to reverse their trajectories so they could come at me from behind.

An old freighter like the *Wah* would have been considered well above average if it had been equipped with the power plant and high-power conduits necessary to mount even one weapons-grade blaster. Two would have been exceptional. But the *Wah* is no ordinary ship. She has six fast-response twin-aperture turrets and the computational capacity to track and engage multiple targets in any direction.

An ordinary vessel of its size would also have required time between shots to recharge its capacitor banks, the duration dependent on the output capacity of its reactor. Only large, multi-reactor ships, or those equipped with extremely-high-output military-grade power plants, can produce anything resembling continuous fire.

The Tattoos would never have committed to a stern chase against an enemy with this capability. Flying behind someone who can lay down accurate fire faster than you can zig and zag is just not healthy.

The four starfighters on my tail soon ceased to be a threat. My problems lay ahead.

One of the massive warships had positioned itself directly between me and D'Orneo's flagship, and the other was in the process of coming around the planetoid, where it would soon be able to parallel my course. Either one by itself was more than capable of turning one little freighter, no matter how tricked out, into a radioactive cloud of debris without breaking a sweat. If I got caught between the two of them, D'Orneo's wish might still come true no matter what I could do.

Charging head-on into such a precarious predicament just didn't seem like my best course of action. Fortunately, I had an alternative available to me that very, very few others in my situation have ever had. The same tremendous computer capacity that can allow me to hack a hacker-proof AI can also be employed to calculate a very precise hyperspace micro-jump.

As I'm sure you're aware, one of the peculiarities of hyperspace travel is that it is much easier to plot a course over interstellar distances than it is one of only a few million miles. What you may not know is that the main factor behind this is the speed at which the continuous calculations that are required to keep a vessel in that quasi-dimension can be performed. Most computers are simply incapable of reacting to the millions of ever-changing variables fast enough to bring a ship out before it has covered the distance best described by the length of time it takes light to cross. And I'm not talking light-seconds or light-minutes, either. There's a reason hyperspace isn't used for in-system travel. Jumps covering light-hours are usually considered the minimum distance possible.

Now don't get me wrong - what I did was by no stretch of the imagination safe. Any of a million things could have gone wrong. If Sam had known I was planning it I'm sure he would have tried to stop me. I just really, really didn't like my chances against those two warships.

Well, obviously it worked. I'm still here to talk about it, right? That being said, I do not recommend that anyone ever try this. Unless, maybe, you have a spare military-grade supercomputer laying around. A micro, micro-jump of barely twenty-five miles fried mine.

It was a gamble, but it paid off handsomely. Barely an instant after I did it, I opened up with the three blaster turrets of mine that were capable of firing in the direction of the warship that had been between me and my target but was now behind me. The great vessel had all available power routed to the shields on its bow, which was pointed at where I had been. There is no way my blasters could ever have penetrated that defense. The good news was that left the warship's stern woefully under-protected. My concentrated fire punched right through the minimal shielding covering its engines and totally destroyed both its normal-space drive and one of its hyperspace motivators.

That made two ships unable to flee the system.

The one I really wanted was just ahead of me, and I was closing in on it fast. In a matter of less than a minute I would be close enough that my blaster discharges wouldn't lose cohesion - in other words, I'd be within weapons range.

I would have been, had it not chosen that very moment to transition itself into hyperspace.

Just like that, D'Orneo and Mela were gone. By the time my brain processed the fact that their ship was no longer there, they were already a light-year or more distant and getting ever farther away with every passing second.

I was a mere millisecond away from engaging my own hyper-drive and giving chase to them when I realized I had to let them go.

Oh, it was hard, so very hard, to not think the command it would take to follow them, but I knew I couldn't. Rescuing Mela and bringing D'Orneo to justice were not the most important tasks vying for my attention just then, as much as I wished otherwise.

Destroying the star killer had to come first.

If I'd been less emotional I would have gone after it first. It, after all, was the real threat. Soon to be capable of wiping out entire star systems, it should have been my only priority all along. But did I do the logical thing and go for it directly? No, I chose, without even being aware that I was making the decision, to pursue Mela and the villain who had kidnapped her instead.

And by doing so, it was possible that I'd not only lost Mela and D'Orneo but had also condemned JD, the planet Alphum and all my family to a fiery death, for the DISK made its own escape into hyperspace before I could change course and get close enough to engage it.

CHAPTER 10

It is just not normally possible to track a vessel through hyperspace. The fabric of that pseudo-spatial realm restores itself within milliseconds after the passage of a ship through it, leaving no trail for anyone to follow.

Unless the pursued ship is leaving breadcrumbs behind and the follower is able to sniff them out.

There are very few mobile ansibles in the galaxy, and it requires both vessels to have one to make a tracking system. Unfortunately, JD was aboard the DISK, not D'Orneo's ship.

And, despite my wishing it were otherwise, I knew which one I must, at all costs, not let escape.

I departed the unnamed system in pursuit of the DISK. Imperial Naval vessels were en-route there but were still almost three weeks away. Perhaps the two vessels I damaged would still be there, perhaps not. I really didn't care. Mela was in the sadistic clutches of that depraved madman, facing torture and enslavement, and it was all my fault.

And there was nothing I could do about it.

I was in a deep funk and nothing I did could pull me out of it. I drove myself to exhaustion exercising and practicing both armed and unarmed combat against holographic enemies, but I kept thinking about how I failed Mela.

I steamed myself like a lobster in the sauna, but I could not sweat out my memory of delivering her to the merciless machinations of that beast in man's flesh. I tried to sleep, but my mind was filled with images of her on his shuttle, writhing under his cruel embrace.

All I could do was follow along and wait for it to re-enter normal space. I had no clue when or where that would be, and the need to constantly be ready to act on a moment's notice was wearing on my nerves. This was made even worse after I reviewed all my scanner logs and came to the conclusion that, while it still needed some more minz coils to be fully operational, it quite possibly could be strong enough already for D'Orneo to risk deploying it.

Time crawled by, day after excruciating day, as I was haunted by terrifying visions of what Mela - proud, strong, unbendable Mela - was undergoing as D'Orneo slowly and torturously broke down her resistance and remolded her into a mindless puppet of his will.

A week passed in this fashion, and then another. Even my ship's computers, as advanced as they are, could only grossly approximately where we were in relation to real space by this time. Since hyperspace has no direct correlation to the real universe, navigating it is extremely complicated. There are no reference points, no road signs or mile markers by which to judge your progress. It is a mathematical abstraction that can be made to temporarily override rational reality, and where a ship goes in and where it emerges are entirely up to the computer running its numbers. And I had no access to that computer.

I could monitor the passage of time, though. I knew, if we were headed in that direction, that we should be approaching the Empire's border.

And then, finally and without warning, it happened.

I'd been spending most of my time on the bridge, waiting for this moment, taking my meals and even sleeping there. I'm well used to long space voyages, and there are many ways to keep one's mind sharp: reading, solving complex equations, and any number of computer-aided activities. And during this interminable chase I had taken to doing most of my physical conditioning there as well. I basically lived there.

But there are still some things I had to momentarily leave

the command center for, and inevitably I was away and occupied elsewhere when the DISK, and thus the *Wah*, finally exited hyperspace.

Okay, I'll admit it. I was in the can, or visiting the head if you prefer. I was sitting on the most important seat in the ship when my day suddenly went from boring routine to life-and-death combat. Fortunately, between my remote control implant and the monitor screen painted on the wall I was able to respond quickly.

And it's a good thing I was, too. As luck, or fate, or whatever you think runs the universe, would have it, it was not just the DISK itself I was facing but the four TA-2 starfighters that had been flying cover for it back in the asteroid field as well. They must have hunkered down inside the huge ship's open framework and come along for the ride.

I had two advantages over them this time, however. The first was that they apparently didn't know they'd been followed. They were all clustered together just inside what was, from my perspective, the south pole of the sphere. If they've been expecting trouble, they would surely have been spread equally around it. And they would have had their shields up.

My other advantage was that I hadn't been confined to a cabin the size of a tiny, cramped closet for over two weeks. I don't care who you are, that has to have a detrimental effect on your combat readiness.

I know it hampered the reflexes of at least one pilot, for he was a bit too slow in activating his shields when I came barreling towards them, blasters blasting. He never did get his shields up, as a matter of fact.

The other three did though, and gave chase as I led them away from the DISK. This was a move intended to keep them from darting back inside its protective embrace, for if it's incredibly powerful shields came online I'd never be able to shoot them down.

The *Wah's* acceleration is far superior to the rate of which it was capable before I bought it, but there is no way it can compare to that of a Tattoo. Outrunning them was out of the question. But that's okay, because I didn't want to escape. They were right where I wanted them.

By concentrating the fire from three blaster turrets onto one fighter I was soon able to overwhelm its shields and revoke its pilot's birth certificate.

The only problem was that the other two were trying to do the same to me.

And it was working.

Without warning, one of the shield generator nodes on the aft port-side suddenly blew out. This, of course, was where the two fighters had been concentrating their fire no matter how much evasive maneuvering I tried. Those little ships are crazy agile, I tell you.

What was so important about this specific location, you may ask? It's simple, really. It was protecting my port-side engine node and hyperspace motivator.

When that node went I was more than a little concerned, for one direct hit to the unprotected engines would severely limit my maneuverability, not to mention eliminate my ability to go hyper.

I kept the *Wah* twisting and turning every which direction, trying to keep her vulnerable flank away from the nipping wolves. Unfortunately, this made it very hard for my targeting computer to keep shooting at them.

The dogfight went on for several minutes that felt more like hours. My inertial compensators were only barely able to cope with the incredible demands being placed on them. I was being slung side to side and up and down, and only my enhanced strength enabled me to hold myself in my seat. The contents of that seat, unfortunately, had no such restraints and were splattered everywhere. Yes, *those* contents.

Finally, the third Tattoo's shields had had enough and it went up in a soundless flash of light. That left only one more.

Something about losing his three companions must have inspired this guy - or gal, I don't actually know which - to fight like never before. The Tattoo flew rings around me, literally. Even with six turrets, one on every side of my ship, and one of the best fire-control computers the Imperial Navy has ever produced, it took another four minutes to finish off this last starfighter.

But it didn't happen before he got a shot in through the weakened shields covering my port engines.

For the first time since I've owned her, the *Wah* was crippled.

(Thanks for blocking that shot, buddy.)

Oftentimes Sam can't tell when I'm being sarcastic, but this time he apparently caught on. ((You are uninjured, and I am capable of towing your ship.))

(Yeah, but you still could have caught that one.)

((It was unnecessary. Every shot that would have led to the destruction of your vessel I did deflect or absorb.))

(Fine. Thanks for that. But now I'm stuck out here who-knows-where with no hyperdrive.)

With the battle finally over, I was at last able to move about the ship. Grabbing a handful of towels, I wet them and quickly took care of the worst of my immediate problem on my way to the bridge. Once there I was able to determine, finally, where in space we were. To my great relief, we were just outside the Sellig system, the home of Herrig's World. Sam would be able to tow the *Wah* in, or I could call for a lift. The navy was probably here already.

But not just yet. I still had one rather large matter of business to tend to.

No, make that *two*, for just then the factory ship that had built the DISK emerged from hyperspace.

Great, and me with only sluggish and coarse maneuverability.

They were there to put the finishing touches on the DISK, no doubt. It would explain why they'd come to this system.

I wasn't going to let them do it, though. No sir, no how, no way.

(Sam, you know you have to destroy that weapon, don't you? And I don't want to hear any talk about it not being an imminent threat or anything like that, either.)

((I had no such protests in mind. I agree that it is too great a danger to be allowed to exist. Would you like me to swallow it?))

After all that I had been through to get to this point, I wanted nothing more than to watch the great buckyball that would have brought down the millennium-old Empire implode in on itself and vanish into nothingness.

The only problem was that JD was still aboard.

Yet to hesitate would be unthinkable. I had the chance to take out the biggest threat the Empire has ever faced, but only if I acted quickly. At any moment the DISK could set its controls for the heart of the sun, and that would be that.

I opened a quicktime comm link to JD. "I need your honest opinion. Is there any chance you'll get into the control routines?"

He's quick, that AI. Just that one question told him exactly what I was facing. "I am afraid not, Sire. Despite all my attempts the system remains impenetrable. I see no alternative other than for you to act while you have the opportunity."

"But there's no way for you to make it out."

"I regret that this is the case, yet you cannot allow the needs of any one to outweigh the needs of many. In as much as I have been able to experience it, I have enjoyed your friendship, Edj. So I ask, as your friend, that you do not hesitate to do what you must. Too many lives will be lost otherwise."

I wanted him to offer me some other option, anything but what we both knew had to be done. But there was simply no time. "You have been a good friend, JD. Your sacrifice will be known throughout the Empire."

"Thank you, Sire. Now strike while you can. Goodbye, Edj."

I did.

I was just relieved that the DISK never had the chance to do what it was designed for. One more interstellar crisis averted, courtesy of your brave, intrepid prince and his faithful android. Why, then, did I feel like I failed so miserably? Mela wasn't the only casualty, after all. Other people lost their lives; she still had hers.

Because you allowed her to accompany you into an unpredictable and volatile situation, the reasonable part of my mind replied.

Very well, then. From now on Prince Edj only works alone.

△△△

I couldn't stand the thought of spending the night alone. The imperial navy had indeed arrived in-system and was already cleaning house in a big way. Based on my reports, as well as other information the ITC had been collecting, hundreds of arrests had already been made and many more were expected. Minzite smuggling was not going to be a problem here for a long time to come.

I should have felt good about all that I accomplished, but it was only a pyrrhic victory. I lost way more than I gained. Nothing short of rescuing Melanada and bringing Lumar D'Orneo to justice would put an end to this whole affair, and that was going to take time. He is out there somewhere, and I'll never stop hunting him down, no matter how long it takes.

But I couldn't even begin the hunt until the navy finished repairing my ship, which I was told would take at least 18 hours.

I called Nicolette and asked if I could buy her that drink. She gladly accepted, and I didn't spend the night alone after all. Sometimes it's good being the prince.

end content Old Empire Archive}

BEFORE YOU GO

Thank you for reading Edj of the Empire: Herrig's World by Timothy Burns. If you enjoyed the book, please do us a favor and leave a review. It can simply be a few lines about what you liked. It goes a long way and we'd really appreciate it. You can learn more about us, our books, and authors here: https://www.chandrapress.com

Join our awesome newsletter and we'll give you a free book! Keep up to date on Chandra Press news and updates and get a free copy of one of our titles: https://www.chandrapress.com/newsletter

Books by Timothy Burns

Edj of the Empire: Herrig's World
Edj of the Empire: Revenant's Omen

Other Sci-Fi Books by Chandra Press

Fusion World: Philanthropy 1 by Joseph Lewis Tamone
Shadow of the Demon: Philanthropy 2 by Joseph Lewis Tamone
Rijel 12: The Rise of New Australia by King Everett Medlin
Return of Anarchy: The Fall of New Australia by King Everett Medlin
Thad Saves the Galaxy by C.T. Fleck
Sworld: The Chronicles of Malick by William Harris
Arachana: The Chronicles of Malick by William Harris
Soteria: The Crisis Forge by Roberto Arcoleo
Mirrors: The Shadow Conspiracy by Sonya Deulina Williams
Moon Hunters by Anya Pavelle